GW01045198

1 9 5108635 9

The Tarot Reading

The Tarot Reading

Mignon Warner

ROBERT HALE · LONDON

ISBN 978-0-7090-8621-5

Robert Hale Limited
Clerkenwell House
Clerkenwell Green
London EC1R 0HT

www.halebooks.com

2 4 6 8 10 9 7 5 3 1

Typeset in 11/14pt Sabon
Printed and bound in Great Britain by
Biddles Limited, King's Lynn

Chapter One

'I'M SORRY, DID I STARTLE YOU?'

Edwina Charles looked up from the flower-bed she was weeding, squinting momentarily into direct sunlight and then shielding her eyes with one of her gardening-gloved hands. The woman standing over her hadn't startled her at all. The clairvoyant had been expecting her. She had known since early morning that at some point during that particular day, a complete stranger would call on her with an unusual request.

'Madame Adele Herrmann?' enquired the woman.

Mrs Charles rose slowly to her feet, dusting the earth from her gloves and then discarding them on the kneeling pad she had been using. 'Yes,' she replied. 'I am 'Del Herrmann.'

'Forgive me for calling on you like this,' the woman then went on quickly. 'I know I should have phoned first and made an appointment, but I was visiting an old friend in the village and you know how it is, we got talking – I don't often get over this way, I hadn't seen my friend in simply ages – and she mentioned you, how good you are at reading the tarot cards and helping people with their troubles, and I thought, why not? – while I'm here—'

She broke off abruptly, as if disconcerted by the clairvoyant's silent contemplation of her and suddenly aware that she was gabbling. 'I'm sorry, I shouldn't have bothered you; it was rude of me. It's just that when my friend mentioned your name, I thought that's it, the very thing. Perfect. A tarot reading.'

The woman's face was flushed, she spoke breathlessly and with a nervous intensity, almost as if there were not a moment to lose.

The clairvoyant averted her gaze from the distinct aura that she could see surrounding the woman which was growing stronger by the minute and was almost blinding in its brightness. She felt increasingly uneasy. Something very serious ailed this woman – or someone close to her. There was something else, too. Her breathless effusiveness was not natural to her: she was using it as a cover. There was something she feared she might reveal; something she wished to conceal which almost certainly meant that the reading she wished to book was not intended for herself. Her high colour could be attributed to the pleasantly warm, early summer's day, but a stronger possibility was the faint whiff of alcohol that Mrs Charles detected on her breath which the peppermint sweet the woman had apparently popped into her mouth moments earlier, was thus far failing to mask.

'Shall we go inside?' Mrs Charles suggested quietly.

'That's very kind of you, but I really must rush. I just want to book a reading and pay for it – if that's all right with you? – and be on my way. It's not for me ... I'm sorry, I didn't mention that, did I? It's a gift.' She looked at the clairvoyant questioningly. 'You'll do a reading?'

'I must know a little more before I give you my answer. You say it is to be a gift—'

'A wedding gift,' the woman interjected, the accompanying quick bob she gave of her head suggesting that this explained everything; she need say no more.

Mrs Charles regarded her thoughtfully, taking in the woman's unlined, rather bland features and her washed-out, hazel eyes which were fixed almost permanently in an unnatural, wide-eyed stare that she used to give either emphasis or credence to every word she uttered. Her mousy-brown, chin-length hair, which was inclined to be frizzy, had a neat centre part and was relatively smooth on the crown of her head, but being naturally bouffant, ballooned out from around her ears in two perfectly formed puff-balls. Her tendency to stare and her unusual hairstyle reminded the clairvoyant of a teddy bear she had owned as a child. The woman was probably in her mid-to-late forties.

'It is my turn now to ask you to forgive me for my rudeness,' said Mrs Charles finally, 'but isn't a tarot reading rather an unusual wedding gift?'

The woman was momentarily thoughtful. 'Yes, I can see why you might think that, but I don't think so, not in the circumstances ... no. It's more of a personal gift ... to the bride. From me to her. She's got these fears, all perfectly unfounded, that something bad is going to happen and that the wedding will be cancelled at the last minute.'

'Has she expressed these fears to you?' asked the clairvoyant.

The woman made a dismissive gesture with one hand. 'Well, I say fears, but there's really only the one big fear – that at the last moment the bridegroom will have second thoughts and call the whole thing off.'

'Surely he must have given her some reason for fearing this,' Mrs Charles pointed out, 'and in which case, I would have thought she would be well advised not to rush into things.'

The woman was shaking her head; her fixed stare became even more intense. 'That's just it, why you must agree to do this reading for her before the big day arrives. You will see how silly she's being, I know you will – it will all be there, in the cards, in black and white, the way I've been told – and you will make her see it, too. She's going to make herself ill, carrying on the way she is, and this should be the happiest time of her life; what she has always wanted, ever since she was a little girl.'

'Again you must forgive me, but how could you, how could anyone, know that she is being silly in this fear of hers that the man she is about to marry doesn't, presumably, return her deep affection for him?'

The woman looked at the clairvoyant levelly for several moments, saying nothing. Her aura flared; momentarily shimmered so strongly that the clairvoyant had to resist the urge to avert her gaze from it.

'She is the most important person in his life,' the woman assured her, again with an accompanying quick bob of her head. 'I know this as only I could. You see, I am the bridegroom's mother.'

Chapter Two

'MRS KELLAR FOUND YOU, THEN,' SAID MRS CHARLES'S BROTHER, Cyril Forbes. He left the loaf of bread that he had picked up for his sister in the village, on her kitchen table, and then, as was his custom, disappeared before she had a chance to thank him, or make some response to what was clearly a statement of fact so far as he was concerned, but meant absolutely nothing to her.

He suddenly reappeared. 'What did she want?' He scowled at the bemused expression on Mrs Charles's face. 'Mrs Kellar,' he said, with more than just a trace of impatience. 'She stopped at my place and asked me where she could find you.'

'A Mrs Sowerby called on me....'

'Her name is Kellar.'

'If you mean the woman who called on me soon after lunch yesterday while I was gardening, Cyril, then the name that woman gave me is Jo – presumably, Josephine – Sowerby.'

'Yes,' he said.

Mrs Charles looked at him. It was going to be one of those days. Any conversation entered into with Cyril today was going to require the patience of a saint. 'Am I to understand that she gave you a different name, Kellar, when she called looking for me?'

'No.'

'I'm sorry, Cyril,' said Mrs Charles patiently, 'but I'm losing the thread of this conversation. Do you think we could start again? If Mrs Sowerby – Kellar,' she corrected herself swiftly, 'didn't give you a name, how do you know what it is?'

'She was the one who was sent out to pay me.'

'Pay you for what, Cyril?'

He gave his sister one of his dark looks. 'For entertaining the children, of course.'

'You gave up Punch and Judy ... what, fifteen years ago?' his sister reminded him.

'Yes,' he said.

Mrs Charles sighed to herself. They were back at square one. Their mother had once told her that the biggest mistake she had ever made with Cyril was to carry him, as a baby in her arms, outside to view the night sky and its constellations. His head had been up there ever since.

'I helped out a friend while you were on holiday in Italy that time,' he said after a moment. He glared at his sister accusingly. 'Your memory is getting terrible, 'Del; I'm sure I told you…. He'd fallen sick and had to go into hospital. He didn't want to disappoint the children, so he asked me if I'd step in and take his place. He was booked to do some magic as well as Punch. Mrs Kellar was there. The little girl with her – her daughter, I guess – screamed and bawled the loudest. She had to drag her out of the house.'

'She was frightened by what Punch does to Judy and the baby – the way he whacks them with a stick?'

'No.'

There was a long silence. Then Cyril said, 'I remembered her name because it was the same as Kellar's.'

Mrs Charles thought for a moment. This was a crucial point in their conversation – such as it was. Come up with the right response and in all probability she would get some, if not a lot of, sense out of Cyril in regard to how he came to know the name of the woman who had called on her yesterday, calling herself Sowerby and wishing to book a tarot reading as a wedding gift.

'Harry Kellar, the American magician who was famous for putting on large stage shows,' Mrs Charles guessed at length. 'I seem to remember your telling me that Howard Thurston stepped into his shoes when Kellar died back in the twenties.'

Cyril nodded.

Mrs Charles took a deep breath. They were making progress. 'You agreed to do some magic for the children, too?'

'Yes, and organize some party games,' he said. 'Only I didn't. Not in the finish. I was paid for my trouble and that was it. I waited for the police to back up their car so that I could drive out – they'd blocked me in – and then I drove straight back home.'

Mrs Charles nodded. 'I see,' she said. She didn't see, but this was the correct response if she wished Cyril to continue and tell her more about the mysterious Mrs Kellar/Sowerby and what the police had had to do with this apparently totally unexpected cancellation of the children's show that he had agreed to give.

'Mrs Kellar wanted me to do a tarot reading,' she explained. 'Not for herself, for the girl her son is about to marry.'

He made no comment.

'I agreed,' Mrs Charles continued, 'although I have to admit that I am not comfortable with the idea. Mrs Kellar had an unusual aura, one I haven't seen in a very long time. I saw extreme violence in it.' She paused momentarily. *And heat*, she thought. *As if the woman were about to spontaneously combust!* She went on, 'This woman has either created havoc in the past among those closest to her, or she is about to in the near future, and if I am right about this obsessively disruptive nature of hers, then in the process, it will cost her her life and not impossibly, that of others.'

'What do you make of it?'

'The obvious answer to that question, Cyril, is that far from wishing well for her daughter-in-law-to-be, as she would have me believe, she dislikes her to such an extent – to the point of it being a driving obsession with her, I would think – that she hopes to do some serious harm to her and prevent the marriage.'

He looked at his sister fixedly. 'With a tarot reading?'

'As I've said, that would be the obvious way of looking at things. But I'm not sure. Her aura, the sparks given off by the raging fire that I saw burning brightly in it, was the only one truth there can be no doubt about.'

'The cards will tell you what's going on.'

'If there is a reading.'

He looked at her questioningly. 'You think it's a hoax?'

'It crossed my mind initially. I'm sure the woman had been

drinking…. But then she insisted on paying me on the spot for the reading, despite my assuring her that this wasn't necessary, she could pay me later. I asked for a contact address or a phone number, but she made some excuse about rarely being at home and said that she would be in touch to arrange a suitable time for the reading. I have no idea where she lives – or who she really is, for that matter. What I actually meant when I said, *"if there's a reading"*, is that first the bride-to-be must want it as much as it would seem her mother-in-law-to-be wants it for her. My feeling is that she would be wise not to accept this particular gift, and not impossibly, she will know this even better than I do. Mrs Kellar – Sowerby, as she told me – said she'd been visiting a friend in the village and that this was how she knew of me.'

Cyril was shaking his head. 'She drove straight in off the motorway; turned round and went back the way she'd come immediately after seeing you.' He was silent for a moment or two. Then he said, 'I think you'll find she lives in Gidding…. At least, that was where I went that time to entertain the children with Punch and some magic and party games.'

'Only you didn't,' Mrs Charles reminded him. She paused for a moment and then added, carefully, 'You turned round after the police arrived and drove straight home.'

'Yes.'

She waited. He nodded and started for the door, the conversation, so far as he was concerned, at an end. But then he paused; stood perfectly still on the spot for a moment or two. 'It probably had something to do with the hearse.' He didn't look at his sister as he spoke: he was thinking out loud; had probably forgotten that he was still in his sister's presence. 'I'd say that was why the party was cancelled and the children were packed off home.'

'What hearse would this be, Cyril?' Mrs Charles ventured.

He looked round at her, the expression on his face one of mild surprise that she should need to ask him this. 'The one standing outside the house when I got there, of course.…'

Chapter Three

LINDA KELLAR SAT BOLT UPRIGHT IN HER BED, LISTENING HARD, HER heart thumping madly.

The house was deathly quiet. The sound she'd heard – something downstairs being knocked over, she thought – wasn't repeated.

She waited a few moments, then slipped out of bed and tiptoed over to the door.

Everything was perfectly still.

So it wasn't her mother coming in. It was too late for it to be her, anyway. She would've come home ages ago; be fast asleep in bed herself by now.

Linda put out a tentative hand and switched on the light.

Nothing happened. Nothing being someone downstairs – a burglar – panicking on discovering that he had woken somebody up and then making a run for it.

The light from Linda's room shone across the passage and into her mother's room, the door of which was open. Her mother's bed hadn't been turned down.

Linda's face darkened. Now what was she supposed to do? If her mother was meeting *him* after she'd finished work for the night at the pub, it was best to keep well clear of the pair of them; but if her mother had passed out again....

Linda left it there. The odds were that her mother was meeting *him* – they'd both been acting like a couple of secret agent morons ever since Barry and Cheryl's wedding plans had got under way – but it was best to make sure. Just in case. She knew where to look for the pair of them, and she would be discreet; keep her distance.

Let them play their stupid games, she thought with a scowl. Who cares what they were up to? Nobody, that's who. Those two lost all credibility ages ago. People started running when they saw them coming. It was embarrassing, but you couldn't tell them they were making fools of themselves. They wouldn't listen; they never had.

It was a clear, warm night. Linda was content to pull on a sweater over her white cotton nightshirt. Besides, the cemetery was less than fifty yards away; she would be there and back – with her mother, if she had been drinking, which was more than likely, and had passed out cold at the graveside again – in next to no time.

A coffee mug was lying broken on the floor as she walked through the kitchen to the back door; the culprit – Horrie, a seriously obese tabby with huge yellow eyes – tiptoed softly round the damage he had caused, all wide-eyed innocence, and followed her outside, then sprinted off, thrilled by this unexpected opportunity to do a little delicious night prowling in the moonlight.

Linda had to climb over a low brick wall to gain access to the cemetery, the iron gates to which were padlocked at night, although why anybody bothered was a mystery to her. It was widely known that the locals – her mother, who was always running late for work, being one of them – used the cemetery as a short-cut to the pub which stood on the corner of a street a little less than a ten-minute-walk from the cemetery, if one took the short-cut, or a good half-hour's walk if one showed a little respect for the dead and had the decency to go the long way round.

Linda was not in the least intimidated by her surroundings. She was far too familiar with the place; had played there as a child, even been responsible, during her early teens, for some of the vandalism that quite a few of the headstones had suffered. Dead is dead: nobody was going to reach up a ghostly hand from inside a grave and drag her down into it. She knew better than most that so far as the Gidding Cemetery was concerned, if there were any worrying to be done, it was the living she needed to focus her mind on late at night like this.

Linda knew exactly where to look. Follow the main path to the chapel, then take the first left…. She never got that far. Soon after starting towards the chapel, she spotted her mother – someone, a woman … who else would it be but her mother? – lying largely on her back, but in a heap. Stoned out of her tiny mind again, the girl thought grimly.

Why, she asked herself crossly, *didn't Barry and Cheryl simply slip quietly away and get married in a register office somewhere and forget all the fuss? Once the deed was done, who knows, her mother might finally settle down.*

Linda knew that wasn't going to happen. Her mother was never going to settle down. *He* wouldn't let her settle down. Not until they had the truth, the whole truth and nothing but the truth.

Whatever they thought that was, thought Linda irritably.

God, it was years ago! Let it rest. Everyone else had.

She had reached the woman lying on the path.

'Look at the state of you, Mum,' she said gruffly, but not unkindly. 'Come on, get up. Time for beddy-byes.'

She bent over her mother. Grabbed her by her right shoulder and gave her a gentle shake, then placed her hands under both of her mother's shoulders and tried to raise her up off the path into a sitting position.

Her mother gave off a strange sound. A soft, sibilant sound of air – wind, perhaps – escaping from her chest.

Linda let go of her mother, mildly shocked by the sound which was the last thing she had expected. *Was that a burp? God, that was totally disgusting! She'd had a skinful tonight all right!*

Her mother fell back limply on to the pathway.

Linda's left hand, which had briefly come into contact with the upper part of her mother's neck, felt inexplicably wet and sticky. She looked at it in the moonlight; had a horrible feeling that it might be blood, but couldn't actually see the dark, glutinous wetness smeared over it as such.

Her mother's face was turned on one side, and Linda tentatively straightened it so that she could look at her face.

Her mother's eyes were closed: she looked pathetic; tired and, worst of all, incredibly old.

Linda stood looking at her. *She wasn't dead, was she?* No, of course not. She'd passed out and fallen over, banging the back of her head. Not for the first time, either.

The thing to do would be to place a hand on her mother's throat and feel for a pulse, but the thought repulsed her: Linda couldn't bring herself to do it. There had never been any close physical contact between them that Linda could remember ... a kiss, or a hug, not so much as a light touch. It was too late to start now.

Besides, what if she couldn't find a pulse?

A shocking thought came to her. She dismissed it. She'd had enough of that sort of thinking, years of it. *I mean, who would want to kill her mother after all this time because she wouldn't stop poking around and asking stupid questions that had no answers and were best left unasked, anyway?* This was— She suddenly realized that her mother's shoulder bag was missing. She looked all round her mother; searched as best she could under her.

Oh, my God!

Her mother had been mugged, the missing bag proved it. It had been bound to happen sooner or later. She *would* walk through the cemetery late at night – and sit talking to gravestones. Some lowlife druggie was bound to pounce on her sooner or later, looking for money to buy his next fix.

A shiver went through Linda and, suddenly nervous, she looked all round her, as if expecting to see someone watching her.

No one was there. She was completely alone.

She looked back at her mother, then reached down and gave her another little shake. 'Mum,' she said. And again, more insistently but in a voice that was beginning to crack with fear, '*Mum*. Come on, get up! You can't stay here all night. Let's go home.'

Her mother made no response.

Chapter four

MRS CHARLES FOLDED THE NEWSPAPER SHE HAD BEEN READING AND then rose from the kitchen table and went into the sitting-room; stood for a few moments at the window, gazing thoughtfully along the road at the car parked outside Margaret Sayer's cottage.

The car belonged to ex-Detective Chief Superintendent David Sayer and as it was his habit to call at the clairvoyant's bungalow for a chat after visiting his elderly aunt, Mrs Charles expected that today would be no exception. What she had to decide between now and then was whether to discuss Jo Sowerby's visit to her three days ago; whether, now that the woman was dead, it wouldn't be better to forget the whole matter.

She was still in two minds about it half an hour later as she and David sat drinking coffee in her sitting-room. David was bemoaning the demands his aunt had been placing on him lately regarding his visits to her and, in particular, the inroads her expectation that he would drop everything and come running was having on his commitments as a security adviser, when abruptly he fell silent. He looked at the clairvoyant levelly for a moment and then he said, 'Something's worrying you. I don't think you've heard a word I've said, have you?'

She smiled. 'You are beginning to sound like my brother.'

'But?' he said when she fell silent.

'I *am* worried,' she admitted. 'And I confess to being rather preoccupied with other matters right now.'

'Something I can help you with?'

'Only perhaps to satisfy my curiosity.... And I'm not at all sure that this isn't something I should walk away from and forget about.'

He inclined his head thoughtfully at her. 'Go on, I'm listening.'

She sighed a little. 'A woman, a complete stranger to me, called on me several days ago, wanting me to read the tarot. She was murdered the night before last; mugged in the Gidding Cemetery.'

David was nodding his head. 'Say no more. Josephine Sowerby – I read about it in this morning's paper. I don't like to speak ill of the dead, but that woman was a right nutter, an accident waiting to happen. She made a habit of taking a short-cut through the cemetery late at night after she'd finished her shift at a nearby pub. The cemetery is a haunt for drug addicts; she was bound to come a cropper sooner or later.'

Mrs Charles looked at him curiously. 'You speak of the woman as if you know rather more about her than what you read in the paper this morning.'

'I wouldn't think there are too many people who live in Gidding, as I do, who haven't heard of Jo Sowerby. She was a heavy drinker, often aggressive with it, and had been making a nuisance of herself for years. To be honest, I don't know much about what's behind it all, only that she had a bee in her bonnet over an accidental death that happened some years ago. Clive Merton mentioned something about it to me once, but only in passing. The detective sergeant who investigated the death used to be on my team – quite a bright young man, but only a DC then; should have had a great career in the force ahead of him but for a serious flaw in his character. He found it difficult to acknowledge his superiors and show due deference to their rank. I had retired by the time this flaw had become a serious problem. He was largely responsible for Jo Sowerby's becoming obsessed about this accidental death. He thought like she did; wouldn't listen to the advice of his superiors who, in this case, apparently, did actually know better than he thought he did. To cut a long story short, he was suspended for insubordination and then finally, he quit. I'm not sure what he's done since – aside from fanning the flames of the fire under Jo Sowerby.'

David paused and looked at Mrs Charles for a moment. There was the hint of a mischievous twinkle in his eye. 'I take it you read the cards for her and didn't spot what lay in wait for her behind one of the cemetery's headstones.'

'I wasn't asked to read the cards for her,' the clairvoyant replied. 'The reading was to be a gift. I had serious doubts about it – whether the recipient would be wise to accept it – and now I am sure of it.'

Mrs Charles was momentarily silent. Then she said, 'I was to read the cards for the girl Mrs Sowerby's son is going to marry.'

David's eyebrows went up questioningly. 'Any particular reason?'

The clairvoyant smiled faintly. 'I would think so. And I doubt that it was the one given to me.'

'Have you heard from the young woman about the reading?'

'No. Hopefully, I won't. As I've said, it was only a few days ago that Mrs Sowerby came to see me; she may not have got round to contacting the girl about what she had in mind for her.'

David looked at the clairvoyant knowingly. 'You really don't want to do this reading, do you?'

She looked at him for a moment. 'I think a comment you made a moment ago sums up my deepest fears about this proposed gift of the late Jo Sowerby – it will serve only to fan the flames.'

Chapter five

LINDA KELLAR SAT WITH HER ELDER BROTHER, BARRY, AND BARRY'S fiancée, Cheryl Baxter, in the living-room of her late mother's home. No one had spoken for a good ten minutes: all three were suffering varying degrees of shock. The police had just left after informing them that Barry and Linda's mother, Josephine Sowerby, had died of natural causes and not as a result of a wound to the base of her skull, the inference here being that a murder investigation would not be launched as had at first seemed likely. According to the pathologist's report, Josephine Sowerby had died of a heart attack. The only crime that had been committed, so far as the police were concerned – and of which there was little, if any, hope of solving – was one of simple theft.

While the real cause of their mother's death was the last thing her son and daughter would have expected, despite her years of hard drinking, it was the precursor to her heart attack that had had the most intense effect on them. Way over the limit when she had left the pub where she had worked three evenings a week as casual bar staff, she had apparently stumbled or tripped over her own two feet, falling and striking her head on one of the granite stones marking out her first husband and their father, Mark Kellar's grave. Linda had learnt the hard way, both with her mother and with her brother and his fiancée, that the least she had to say on any subject touching on family matters the better; she wouldn't have commented, anyway, but of the two of them, she was the one whose shocked silence was the most profound on hearing this aspect of the circumstances leading up to her mother's death.

A close forensic examination by the police of the surrounding area pointed to Jo Sowerby's having got up from the graveside after falling and striking the back of her head, and then staggering to the spot where her daughter had ultimately found her. At some point after suffering a heart attack and collapsing unconscious on to the pathway near the chapel, she had been robbed of her shoulder bag and its contents – whatever money she'd had on her, a debit card and several credit cards, her mobile phone and any jewellery that she might have been wearing – by a person or persons thus far unknown.

'You should've gone looking for her,' said Cheryl, echoing one of Barry's earlier criticisms of his seventeen-year-old sister's behaviour on the night that their mother had died. Cheryl was twenty-five, the same age as Barry; fair-haired, not unattractive, other than for a tendency to scowl, regardless of the circumstances, and at five-feet-three inches in height and tipping the scales at twelve and a half stones, definitely bordering on becoming clinically obese.

'I did go looking for her,' Linda protested. She was close to tears. 'You know I did. How many more times do I have to tell you that I went looking for her the moment I realized she hadn't come home from work? I was fast asleep – it was Horrie who woke me up when he knocked a mug off the kitchen worktop and it smashed on the floor. If it hadn't been for that, it could easily have been morning before I knew she hadn't come home....' Linda's voice tailed off. It was so unfair. Everything was always her fault. She couldn't do anything right.

'You should've gone out earlier, before you turned in for the night,' said Barry. 'Chances are Mum would still be alive if you'd stirred yourself sooner. Had the boyfriend round – what's his name, Ever Ready Eddie? – did you?'

'I'm sure the paramedics could have saved Jo if you'd called an ambulance the moment you found her lying unconscious on the path,' Cheryl cut in, the natural scowl on her chubby face darkening unpleasantly as she looked at Linda.

As if you really care, Linda thought, resisting the urge to scowl back. *You were terrified of Mum*. A note of desperation crept into her voice. 'I've told you: I thought she was sleeping it off, like always. How was I to know she was unconscious? I'm not a doctor.'

Barry gave her a disgusted look. No one could doubt that he and Linda were brother and sister. Physically, they were very alike, with dark-brown eyes, healthy pink cheeks and short, rich chestnut hair that flopped over the right side of their foreheads and curled round their ears. Temperamentally, they were complete opposites. Nothing worried Barry, there was always someone he could find to shoulder the load or blame for whatever went wrong in his life, while Linda was a born worrier who suffered in silence, hugging all the things that troubled her tightly to her chest. They were the same height, five-feet-eight-inches, and had once been identically slim. Less than two months after Barry and Cheryl had moved into the flat they were buying on the other side of town, Barry's waistline had begun to expand alarmingly. His mother blamed the weight increase on the fact that Cheryl wouldn't know a carrot or any sort of fresh vegetable if she fell over one, and that she was addicted to convenience food. Privately, Linda thought the physical alteration in her brother's appearance had nothing whatsoever to do with a change in eating habits and was down to his having moved out of the family home which had inevitably loosened his ties with their mother. Linda sometimes wondered if this hadn't been the prime mover in his decision to set up home with Cheryl who had always been much keener on the idea.

On the other hand, Cheryl was still Cheryl; striking out independently had had no noticeable effect on her: she had continued to hang on to every word Barry uttered and had remained scared stiff, in Linda's opinion, that at any moment he would have second thoughts and dump her. Their mother's death had changed all that. Quite literally overnight, Cheryl wasn't the same person. Gone was the meek little mouse that had hovered in Barry's wake ever since they were children, hopeful of any crumbs that he might care to scatter her way: she now had more to say than both of them put together. Barry either hadn't noticed this, or he didn't care, which puzzled Linda. He had never liked to be pushed and had always lived life at his own pace. Long term, Linda could see Cheryl developing into a problem, not in every way like their mother, but in many respects similar, and then where would Barry run?

'Good God, Linda,' said Barry, taking up where Cheryl had left off. 'You're not a child any more. We thought we could rely on you to look out for Mum.'

'I did look out for her,' Linda protested.

Cheryl made a soft, snorting noise through her nose and rolled her eyes upwards.

'We should've waited a bit longer, until after we were married,' said Barry to Cheryl. 'It was too soon for me to move out and leave Mum with Linda.'

I'm sitting here, right beside you, Barry: I haven't got up and left the room! Linda wanted to scream at her brother; but instead, she muttered, half to herself, 'I couldn't be with her twenty-four hours a day. No one could. Not even you, Barry,' she added, in a bitter undertone. 'You know what Mum was like.'

He gave her a look. 'I've given the police a list, including a description, of the jewellery she would have been wearing,' he said. 'A gold St Christopher on a chain – she always wore that, didn't she?' (He directed this question at his fiancée and not to the person best placed to answer it.) 'A silver-coloured bracelet watch and the diamond cluster ring Dad gave her. I told them she didn't wear a wedding ring: she ditched the one Sowerby gave her when he walked out on us. They told me they might get lucky with Dad's ring, that's if whoever stole it tries to pawn it.'

'She wasn't wearing it,' said Linda. 'You'll have to tell them.'

'What do you mean?' Cheryl actually bristled; looked quite hostile. 'She always wore it.'

'She took it to the jewellers at the top of Prince Street to have it resized,' said Linda. 'The knuckle on her ring finger was swollen – she said she had arthritis in it.'

'When was this?' Cheryl demanded to know.

'A week ago.' Linda shrugged. 'A bit longer, perhaps. I can't remember.'

'You're sure about this?' asked Barry.

Cheryl looked at him. 'I wouldn't worry about it, Barry.' She flashed a scowl at Linda. 'You know what Linda's memory is like. I'm sure your mother was wearing it.'

Cheryl's tone of voice was patronizing. Linda found it sickening and, frightened that it would show on her face and start a row, she got up abruptly and walked out of the room. Barry and Cheryl stared at one another in wide-eyed silence as they listened to her climbing the stairs.

'Where does she think she's going?' asked Cheryl at length. She shook her head at her fiancé. 'We're not finished here yet, Barry. There are things we must discuss.' She looked and sounded quite put out. 'There's something wrong with that girl. She's far too deep.'

Chapter Six

LINDA KNEW INSTINCTIVELY THAT IT WOULD NOT BE HER BROTHER she could hear climbing the stairs.

She was sitting on the edge of their mother's bed with a small, blue metal document box nestling in her lap. The gift card she was looking at she quickly slipped beneath her right buttock, out of sight.

As Cheryl entered the room, Linda looked round at her and said, 'Mum hadn't picked up her ring. She would've had to give them this to get it back.'

Cheryl took the jeweller's receipt Linda handed to her. She read it; as she finished, she angled her left hand slightly and looked thoughtfully at the diamond engagement ring Barry had given her. Linda had a fair idea of what was going through Cheryl's mind, recalling how her mother had mocked Barry for the smallness of its stone with the remark that one would need a magnifying glass to see it. The meek little mouse she was back then, Cheryl had not dared to comment, but Linda had seen the look that came fleetingly into her eyes: she had not been amused.

'I'll pick this up tomorrow during my lunch hour,' said Cheryl.

Linda said nothing. She closed the lid of the document box and then, when Cheryl held out a beckoning hand to her, passed it to her without comment. Cheryl lifted the lid and glanced into it, then, tucking it under an arm, she wandered over to the window and looked out over Jo Sowerby's unkempt back garden.

'I'm surprised the neighbours have never complained and got someone from the council to come round and take a look at that

24

mess out there,' she commented after a moment. 'We are going to have to do something about it.'

It had been in its present state for as long as Linda could remember. Barry hadn't lifted a finger to tidy it up, it had never bothered him that nothing was ever done out there. Her mother rarely went out the back, and the work involved in restoring it to some semblance of a garden was way beyond Linda's capabilities.

'Why?' she asked. *Silly question*, she thought. She was already one giant step ahead of Cheryl; knew exactly what was going through her mind at that moment. Cheryl was an estate agent, already assessing, in her estimation, the worth of the property which she undoubtedly intended to pressure Barry to put up for sale.

Cheryl had turned from the window and was casting a practised eye over the ceiling. She let her gaze drift downwards and then travel slowly round the walls of the room.

She smiled patronizingly at Linda; made no reply. Then, moving to the door, she paused and said, casually, 'Your mother left a will, I suppose.'

Linda shrugged. 'Mum didn't discuss that sort of thing with me. Ask Barry.'

Oh, I intend to, thought Cheryl, a small, grim smile playing on her lips.

Linda waited until she heard the murmur of voices downstairs before deciding it was safe to take another look at the gift card she was sitting on.

She wasn't sure why she didn't want Cheryl to see it. Or her brother, for that matter. *Because they would mock her?* Probably. She had managed only a quick glimpse at the handwriting on the card, her mother's, before she'd heard the footsteps on the stairs, and was pretty sure of its intention. Her mother could be very cruel, really nasty when she'd been drinking.

It was a flowery card, devoid of verse and left blank for the sender, or in this instance, the giver of the gift that accompanied it, to write his or her own message inside it.

Her mother hadn't quite finished all that she'd had to say, which didn't really matter. Linda got the message.

She looked at the business card that her mother had paper-clipped to it.

As a schoolgirl, Linda had spent two weeks during the summer holidays one year, working as a bird scarer in a farmer's field in the village of Little Gidding, but she knew nothing of the clairvoyant, Madame Adele Herrmann, who lived there and who apparently read tarot cards for useless people like her who couldn't make up their minds about what to do next with their lives.

This is the time to make decisions and do the right thing. Then with a clear head and pure heart, move on with no shadow of doubt hanging over you. This, a reading of the tarot cards, is my special gift to you at this momentous time in your life; use it and set yourself free of the

That was as far as her mother had got.

Linda slipped the two cards back into the envelope, which her mother hadn't got round to addressing, and then gazed at it steadily, almost as if in so doing, her name would suddenly materialize on it.

She wasn't actually thinking about the card, or the unaddressed envelope and the gift of a tarot reading; her thoughts were occupied with her mother's ring and whether or not Barry would bother to let the police know that she wasn't wearing it.

Cheryl would, of course, make the decision for him to do the right thing. Whatever that was in her book.

But who was going to make the decision for me to do the right thing? Linda asked herself anxiously. She should really speak to the police, too; tell them they had it all wrong about her mother.

She couldn't do that, though, could she? No way. If she told them they'd made a terrible mistake, then everyone would know that she'd pretended all this time and wonder why.

No, they wouldn't wonder why. They would know why, and then....

And then what she'd hoped had finished with her mother's death, would start all over again. *He'd* start it all over again.

She couldn't face it.

Questions and more questions and never any answers because....

Because there weren't any answers: it was all in her mother's head. It had only ever been in her head. *His,* too. *He* couldn't or wouldn't see it, either. They both kept asking the same questions, never getting the answers, or rather the one answer they wanted, but hoping that one day someone would give it to them.

There was no answer other than for the one they had already been given by everyone: they could have asked the same question a thousand times and gone on asking it, and it would still have been the same.

Best not to do anything, she thought. The police knew what they were doing.

Linda began to tremble, the first sign of a panic attack. And worse. Tonight she would have the dream....

Chapter Seven

'I'M SORRY, BUT I DON'T THINK THERE'S A LOT I CAN TELL YOU THAT you don't already know about Jo Sowerby's death,' confessed David Sayer when he called on Edwina Charles the following week. 'There wasn't anything suspicious about it. She suffered a fatal heart attack; she wasn't mugged: the head wound turned out to be a bit of a red herring. Her shoulder bag was stolen, either while she was lying unconscious on the cemetery path, or after she'd actually died, and so far nothing's turned up. Nobody's tried to use her credit cards, I mean. Her mobile phone was taken – that's probably already been sold on – and a couple of pieces of jewellery, nothing particularly valuable, were also stolen. They haven't been sighted, either.'

'How did she get the wound to her head?'

'That happened earlier. She missed her footing while she was visiting her first husband's grave and fell backwards, striking her head on a stone. She was in the habit of taking a short-cut home through the cemetery after finishing her shift at a local pub for the night, and made a point of stopping and having a nice long chat with him. The police knew about this after speaking to her daughter following some trouble a while back between her mother and some kids who were hanging out in the cemetery one day as she was walking through it. These kids knew her – such was her reputation around town for a fondness for a glass or three of the amber nectar – and they started taunting her and calling her names. She gave as good as she got – in fact, in this instance, a lot better than she got! She lashed out at one of the boys with a fist and broke his nose. She finished up being arrested

– this was after the boy's parents had made a formal complaint – but got off with a caution when they decided not to press charges.'

'Do you know if she'd been drinking the night she died?'

He nodded. 'She finished up at the pub where she worked part-time somewhere around eleven o'clock, and one of the regulars who walked with her as far as the pub's car-park, told the police that she'd had a job to walk in a straight line. She kept tripping over her feet and he'd had to grab her by an arm more than once to steady her when it looked as if she might have been going to pitch head first on to the ground.'

'Was it Chief Superintendent Merton who gave you this information?'

Again David nodded. 'It was. This is the official police version of events.'

'What did he have to say about the wound to her head?'

'Not a lot. It's as I've told you, she was well known in the town. The incident with the kids in the cemetery wasn't the only time she'd found herself in trouble with the law. The police were called out on a number of occasions when she'd been drinking heavily and had started behaving aggressively, usually in shops.'

Mrs Charles looked at him thoughtfully. 'You said something the other day about her having had some sort of obsession about an accident. Do you know what that was all about?'

'I mentioned it to Clive and he said it was all to do with a girl who was accidentally drowned ten or eleven years ago in what was known then as "the gravel pit" – a local haunt for young people at the time, those wanting a quick fag behind their parents' backs … and goodness only knows what else besides! The gravel pit and the patchy woodland surrounding it have since been levelled and developed; built over with modern, affordable council housing. A big mistake. The area was a flood plain and still is – the whole site floods regularly every time there's prolonged heavy rain. This was how the girl came to drown. She and her friends were messing about there late one afternoon after school and she somehow tumbled down the side of the pit. Shallow water had collected in the bottom of it after some recent heavy rain and she apparently landed heavily, face down. There'd been some sort of spat between her and her best friend and her friend had gone off alone in a huff, saying she was going home. By the time someone thought it might be a good idea to go after her and make sure she was OK, it was too late; she was dead. Jo Sowerby and the young detective sergeant I mentioned the other day have always said that this was when she died and not earlier – after she had walked off alone, that is – and that she was deliberately pushed into the pit.'

'Do you happen to know by whom?'

'By the dead girl's best mate, the one she'd had her spat with who later decided to go after her. Cheryl – I'm not sure of her last name ... Baxter, I think.'

Chapter Eight

LINDA LET OUT A SMALL SCREAM, HALF STIFLING IT WITH THE HAND that she placed quickly over her mouth.

'I'm so glad you're pleased to see me, Linda,' said the man sitting in her mother's favourite armchair. He rose casually to his feet, clasping his hands behind him and then rocking back a little on his heels. He was in his early forties, tall, with a close-shaved head and a face like carved granite, Linda had always thought, a face that rarely, if ever, showed any emotion whatsoever. 'I thought it was time we had a little chat.'

'How did you—?' Linda was going to ask how he had got into the house, but the answer was obvious. Her mother had given him a key; she probably often came home of a day and found Roy Adams waiting for her like this.

'What do you want?' she asked him. She looked and sounded like a small, truculent child.

'The same thing your mother wanted, of course,' he replied. He looked at Linda levelly. 'Just because she's gone doesn't mean that's the end of it.'

He smiled to himself at the look in Linda's eyes. He knew she was scared of him; she'd been scared of him ever since the day her mother had brought her to his home and they had found him sitting out on his patio, picking off crows with his shotgun. Well, tough. She was going to get a lot more scared of him before he'd finished. He was going to make sure of it. Nobody played games with him and got away with it, and certainly not this kid who had always given him the impression that she was half brain-dead.

Linda felt a little ripple of fear go through her. She was sure he saw it. She swallowed quickly. 'My brother's fiancée will be here soon with some people – prospective buyers – who want to look over the house. I don't think it'd be a good idea for her to find you here—'

'Selling the house, is she?' He was silent for a moment. Then he said, simply, 'H'm.'

He squared his shoulders, but made no move to leave; simply stood looking at her. He wasn't a police officer now, hadn't been with the force for nigh on ten years, but he still looked and behaved like one. He was always so sure of himself; just looking at him made Linda feel sick to her stomach. She hadn't noticed it until that moment, but the room reeked of the aftershave he used, the same one he was using that day when she was eleven years old and she'd been made to watch him shooting crows. Its aroma was beginning to burn the back of her throat; she felt as if her airways were closing over.

The last she'd heard, he was working as a security guard in a local supermarket. He never lasted long anywhere, though, and had probably changed jobs several times since then. There was always something wrong, and usually the same thing: he couldn't get along with his workmates, particularly those in a senior position to whom he had to answer. He thought he knew better than everybody and she just wished that he had never come into their lives, and that he would go away now and leave them alone.

'Your mother asked me to meet her on the night she died,' he said after a moment. 'Did you know that, Linda?'

Linda made no comment. Her heart was thumping; she was sure he could hear it and was enjoying the effect he was having on her.

'After she'd finished up at the pub for the night.... In the usual place, the cemetery,' he said after a small pause.

He waited for her to say something; smiled to himself when she remained silent.

'I didn't make it ... meet her, I mean. My car broke down halfway there: I tried to hire a taxi, but they were all out on calls. I had to text her on her mobile phone to let her know what had happened, and that we'd have to meet some other time.'

'Her mobile was stolen,' Linda blurted out. Almost immediately, she asked herself why she'd bothered to tell him this. She sounded childish, even to her own ears. And what difference did it make?

It was his turn to be silent. He pursed his lips a little; nodded his head slightly. Then he said, 'Your mother phoned me earlier that day and said she had something she wanted to tell me. She sounded excited; wouldn't tell me what it was over the phone.'

'Mum didn't get excited ... ever,' said Linda.

'I know,' he said, amused at the petulance he could hear in her voice. 'That's what made me curious. She got angry, yes – abusive ... yes, that too, frequently; was hostile most of the time. H'm ... now what, I wonder, could it have been that changed the habits of a lifetime and made her excited?'

'Don't ask me. Mum never discussed anything with me.'

He smiled to himself, his unwavering gaze never leaving her face.

'Leave us alone,' she said.

'Unfortunately, Linda, I can't do that. And you know I can't, don't you?'

'What do you mean?' She knit her eyebrows in a tense frown; her heart pumped even harder. *He knows*, a little voice inside her cried.

'I mean that nonsense about your mother cracking her head open on or near your father's grave.'

'That's what happened,' she said defensively. 'The police said—'

He cut across her voice. 'Your mother never went anywhere near your father's grave, Linda.'

'You don't know that—'

He went on as if she hadn't spoken.

'She hated Mark Kellar in life and even more in death. His grave is the last place she'd be seen – if you'll forgive me for saying it – dead!'

'You know that because you were there, do you?' Linda shot back at him, before she could stop herself. Her stomach muscles were taut with dismay: where had she got the courage to say such a thing, and to him, of all people? Provoking this particular man was the worst thing she could do, worse even than provoking her mother. They both thought they were never wrong and that everyone else was thick and stupid. Humour him and maybe he'd go....

'She didn't really like men, did she?' he continued. 'Hated Sowerby, I understand, even more than she hated your father. Do the police know that, do you think?' He paused and looked at Linda thoughtfully. 'I've often wondered, you know, why she bothered to get married.'

'The police won't listen to you. Nobody listens to you!' She wanted to shout at him, '*You're not a bloody copper any more, Roy Adams. You've no right to be talking to me like this.*' But she didn't. She did what she always did when she found herself being backed into a corner; said nothing.

Her silence amused him, but nothing showed on his face. 'Yes, Linda? There's something else you'd like to say? Shall I tell you what I think? I think your mother died because of this exciting something she wanted to tell me. What's more, I think she was excited for once in her life because she'd finally uncovered something that would help her, *us*, to prove what we've always known to be the truth.'

Linda was staring so hard at him, spots were forming before her eyes. *You're mad*, she thought.

'So now it's down to the two of us, Linda,' he said. 'You and me. I'd like to include your brother in our noble quest, but we can't do that, can we? Not now that he's getting married; not without compromising our endeavours to reach the truth.'

'Barry's never believed you about Cheryl.' There was a slight quiver in Linda's voice as she spoke. 'He loves her and she loves him. He knows she didn't do it – what you and Mum say she did; she couldn't be so horrible. They're really happy—' She was going to add, *for the first time in years*, but then that would have been disloyal to her mother, so she bit her tongue and said instead, 'Why can't you leave us alone?'

Ex-Detective Sergeant Roy Adams looked at her for a moment, then walked to the door where he paused and then, without looking back at her, he said, 'Sorry, Linda, that's something I can't do. And you know what? It's your fault. You really shouldn't have lied to the police about your mother's visits to your father's grave. That was not only very naughty of you, but also just a tad stupid, bearing in mind the risk you were taking. You see, Linda, there's always the chance that there's someone out there who knows you lied and might wish to point out to the police the error of their thinking....'

The spots before Linda's eyes multiplied sickeningly; Linda thought she was going to faint. She knew what Roy Adams was really telling her. He was going to blackmail her. Blackmail her into doing what he wanted.

Or else!

Chapter Nine

'THAT'S BLACKMAIL,' SAID DETECTIVE CHIEF SUPERINTENDENT CLIVE Merton. He glared at David Sayer, his florid complexion darkening dangerously. It was an extremely warm day, the air-conditioning unit had broken down and Merton's office was like a little oven. Both men were perspiring heavily.

'Take it or leave it,' said David.

'You and Jean will spend the whole of Sunday with us? You won't leave me alone with the sister-in-law for a second?'

'Not even for a nanosecond,' said David, smiling to himself. Few people intimidated the chief superintendent, his martinet, civil rights activist sister-in-law being one of them. It was going to be a difficult day, but as David had explained to his wife, Jean, when briefing her of his plan to enlist Merton's aid on Mrs Charles's behalf, all in a good cause.

'All right, so what is it that Madam Marvellous wants me to do this time?' sighed Merton.

'Well, to be honest, it's really more on my behalf. Mrs Charles hasn't actually asked me outright to approach you....'

'But,' said Merton when David paused.

'There's something wrong, something troubling her about the circumstances of Jo Sowerby's death. I saw it in her eyes the last time I called on her. Just get someone to take another look, Clive – as a personal favour to me, if you like.'

Merton sighed again. 'I'm not going to tell you there's been a terrible mistake and that Jo Sowerby was murdered, if that's what you and Madam Marvellous would like to hear. She died of a heart attack, David. Pure and simple.'

David said nothing.

'So our esteemed clairvoyant thinks otherwise, does she?' Merton leaned forward over his desk and rested his head in his hands. 'I'm not going to ask why, my blood pressure won't stand it. Why doesn't she get out her crystal ball and save us all a whole lot of trouble?'

'You've got to admit that it's a strange business,' said David.

Merton raised his head and looked at him. 'There's nothing strange or unique about a heart attack. Even you've managed to have one.'

'Just take another look, Clive. Not at the actual cause of Jo Sowerby's death, but at the whole picture.'

'Would it be asking too much to know exactly what I'm supposed to be looking for?'

David looked at him for a moment. 'How about grounds for murder?'

Chapter Ten

LINDA CAUGHT A BUS INTO LITTLE GIDDING AND THEN RETRACED THE last leg of her journey, walking back from the village centre, out along the road towards the motorway.

She walked straight past the clairvoyant's bungalow and then on, almost up to the spot where the road merged into the roundabout that gave on to the motorway. Turning back, she was once again resolute when it came to choosing whether or not to pause and then walk up to Mrs Charles's front door and ring the bell. She carried on towards the village, disgustedly flinging the business card she'd been clutching ever since stepping off the bus a little over half an hour earlier, into the hedgerow.

She didn't know what had possessed her to think this was a good idea.

'Miss,' somebody called out to her. 'I think you dropped this.'

She gave a start and looking round quickly, saw a short, very thin, middle-aged man with a pair of binoculars strung round his neck, stepping through a gap in the hedgerow. He was holding the discarded card out to her.

'You've walked past the place you've been looking for twice,' he said, walking up to Linda. 'You'll find Madame Herrmann – Mrs Charles, as everybody round here knows her – back there.' He pointed to the clairvoyant's bungalow. 'That's her you can see looking out of her sitting-room window at us,' he added, raising his grey linen hat in greeting at the woman watching them.

'I'll walk you over there, if you like,' he offered. 'I'm hunting the blue moth again today; couldn't believe my eyes when I sighted one in the wood at the bottom of Mrs Charles's garden yesterday afternoon. They're rare, you know. Getting rarer by the year.'

Linda let Stan North, Little Gidding's amateur entomologist and weather forecaster, who was renowned locally for lurking surreptitiously but innocuously in the hedgerows, take her fatherly by an elbow and guide her carefully across the road as if it were a busy London thoroughfare.

Mrs Charles was waiting for them in the open doorway of her home.

'Young lady's been looking for you, Mrs Charles,' Stan North explained, again raising his hat to her and then turning to leave.

'Thank you, Mr North,' said the clairvoyant with a smile. She extended an arm to Linda. 'Please, come in.'

Linda had no idea why she did it, but she held out the clair-voyant's business card, almost as an apology for what she was about to say. 'I don't have an appointment—'

The clairvoyant took the card from her without comment, looked at it for a moment, and then, indicating towards her sitting-room, she said, 'Please go through and sit down. I'll be with you in a moment or two. I'll make us some tea.'

Linda did as she was told; sat tensely on the edge of the sofa nearest the window, trying to make up her mind what she was going to say. Was no wiser ten minutes later when she heard the clairvoyant's approaching footsteps on the bare parquet flooring in the hall.

'I wasn't told when to expect you,' said Mrs Charles, as she entered the room with the tea tray, 'but I was given to understand that a tarot reading was to be a gift.'

Linda breathed a sigh of relief. This was going to be easier than she'd thought. 'I haven't been able to make up my mind what to do for the best – for the future, that is. I'm not very good at making decisions. I usually put things off ... you know, until it's too late to do anything about it – whatever it is that I have to make up my mind about.'

Mrs Charles poured the tea. 'How are the wedding arrangements coming along?'

Linda scowled. 'I'm actually sick to death of the whole business. It's all they ... I mean, Cheryl, really – Cheryl, my brother's fiancée – talks about and it's getting on my nerves. I just wish they'd hurry up and get on with it. I think it's even beginning to get on Barry's nerves, too – Barry's my brother. He thought they should wait a bit ... you know, because of what happened to our mother – you know about that, I suppose – but Cheryl said it wasn't an option. I guess she's right. They can't really afford to cancel everything at such short notice and lose the deposits they've paid for the church and the reception, not to mention their honeymoon in Bali which is going to cost them a fortune.'

Mrs Charles looked up at her thoughtfully as she replaced the teapot on the tray, but she made no comment. The girl was beginning to gabble, hardly pausing for breath and not bothering to wait for a response to her statement concerning her mother, a sure indication that she was very nervous about something. That she had claimed the gift of the tarot reading for herself, knowing that her mother had intended it for someone else? 'Your mother didn't give me your name when she called on me about her gift.'

'It's Linda. I found the gift card among my mother's things after she'd died. She said she wanted me to do the right thing and finally make up my mind about what I wanted to do with my life.'

'Your mother actually told you this?'

Linda shook her head. 'She wrote it all down on the card – what she wanted me to do. She didn't get to finish it.... Knowing her, there'd have been a lot more she'd wanted to say and she'd needed to think about it for a bit. I haven't told anybody – I mean, about the gift – that I was coming to see you today.'

'Why is that, Linda?'

The girl's expression soured. 'They're always picking on me – Barry and Cheryl ... Mum was, too, for not being able to make up my mind and being such a wuss about everything. It would only make things worse if they knew I was coming to see you – a clairvoyant, I mean – and asking you to make up my mind for me.'

'I can't do that for you, Linda. I can only read the tarot and from what I see in the cards, guide you, I hope, in the right direction. The ultimate decision over what to do with your life will and must be yours.'

Mrs Charles watched the frown on the girl's face deepen. 'Is that so much of a problem, Linda?'

'Will you—?' Linda hesitated. 'I don't want my fortune told; that isn't what my mother wanted.'

'What do *you* want, Linda?'

'I want—' Again Linda hesitated. 'I'm afraid,' she admitted.

'Of the future, what it holds for you?'

'Just afraid,' she confessed. She took a deep breath. 'Of every-thing....' She momentarily faltered, then blurted out, 'Of the dream. It's no use telling me my fortune; I don't have a fortune, a future. That's why I can never make up my mind. There's no point, you see. I know I'm not going to live for very much longer.'

Mrs Charles took Linda's teacup from her and then crossed to the antique writing bureau standing in a corner of the room.

Linda's eyes followed her anxiously.

Without looking at her, the clairvoyant took a pack of tarot cards from the bureau and then she said, very quietly, 'Tell me about the dream, Linda.'

Chapter Eleven

LINDA LOOKED DOWN AT HER HANDS WHICH WERE CLASPED TIGHTLY in her lap. Her heart was racing. She had never spoken of the dream to anyone before: she wasn't sure she could now.

Sensing the girl's growing distress, Mrs Charles said, quietly, 'Tell me about the first time you had the dream, Linda.'

'I can't remember when that was,' the girl replied.

'When you were a child, perhaps?'

'I don't know. Except....' Linda paused for a moment. 'I'm a child in the dream. At least I think I am. I'm excited, happy ... waiting for something special to happen.' She looked up at the clairvoyant with a puzzled frown. 'And then it all changes. I'm not excited and happy any more. Everything is grey and scary. Something – I don't know what it is, this part is never in the dream, but something happens that changes everything.'

'Are you alone in this dream?'

Linda thought for a moment before answering. 'No. There are lots of other people all around me, but I never see their faces. I can't see them because they are sort of grey and blurred. Really scary.' She fell silent, turning her head to gaze out of the window. After a few moments, she went on, in a strangely distant voice, 'We – all of us – are waiting for ... for someone, I think. I'm not sure.... And then the next thing, there are all these flowers.... They are everywhere.' She made a strange gulping sound, covering her nose and mouth with one hand. 'I can't breathe ... the flowers ... their strong perfume makes me feel sick. And then there's all this screaming—' She broke off, looking at Mrs Charles with eyes that were stark with fear.

'Somebody is laughing. It's a horrible, mad sound. It terrifies me.'

She looked out of the window again and then round at Mrs Charles with a perplexed frown. 'I try to see who is laughing – I think it's a woman – but I can't see her face, either. And then I'm screaming. I'm being dragged through a very big doorway towards a long, black car. It's someplace I don't want to go and the car that's waiting is going to take me there.' She made another curious, gulping sound. 'I start to scream even louder, so loud it makes my ears ring ... this is in the dream. I can't stop myself. All the grey, scary faces are looking at me ... their eyes....' Linda closed hers tightly, swallowing hard. 'Suddenly I see their eyes, burning into me, hating me, wanting me to stop screaming and hurry up and get into the black car and be driven away from that place.'

Linda started to gulp in air. She was visibly beginning to shake; close to hyperventilating, the clairvoyant suspected. Having reached this point, and out of concern for the girl's well-being, she would normally have drawn a line under this line of questioning and moved in an entirely different direction, but there was no alternative, she had to probe further about the dream before reading the tarot. She was convinced that the source of the girl's problem, and inevitably the solution to it, lay in this recurring dream and its meaning.

'Tell me about the flowers, Linda,' said Mrs Charles in a soft voice. 'Describe them to me.'

'I can't ... just thinking about them makes me feel as if I am going to choke.'

'Are they bunches of flowers; pretty posies, perhaps?'

Linda said nothing for some moments. Then, looking at Mrs Charles with another perplexed frown, she said, 'Some are ... bunches of flowers, I mean. The others....' She closed her eyes for a moment. 'One of them ... it spells out someone's name. I know it's a name, but I can't read it. I think it might be my name.'

'And the black car waiting outside, Linda?' asked the clairvoyant in a quiet voice.

Linda eyes snapped open and widened. She was visibly

shocked. 'It's a hearse, isn't it?' she whispered. 'And it's waiting for me.'

Stan North wasn't an observant man when it came to the ordinary everyday things of life, like motor cars, for example, but he saw this one, principally because it almost ran him down as he stepped from the verge on to the roadway after his latest foray in the hedgerows while hoping for a glimpse of another beautiful blue moth like the one he had spotted yesterday.

A sharp warning blast from the car's horn and an angry glare from the bald-headed male driver snapped him out of his reverie and he stood, momentarily rooted to the spot, and not just a little in shock, watching the car as it drove on. The girl he had escorted up to Edwina Charles's front door the best part of an hour and a half ago, was walking along the road roughly fifty yards ahead of him, back towards the village.

As Stan recovered his composure, the car that had almost run him down drew up alongside the girl: the driver leaned across the front passenger-seat and spoke to her through the open window. She had paused as his car had drawn to a halt, and in response to whatever it was that he was saying to her, she was shaking her head vigorously. She spoke to the driver, but she didn't appear to be having a lot to say to him.

Something about the girl's stance, the way she kept shaking her head at whatever it was that the man was saying to, or asking her, her short responses, didn't seem quite right to Stan, but only vaguely. A dragonfly, the *Libellula depressa* or Broad-bodied Chaser – one with a pale blue abdomen which identified it as being a male – had crossed Stan's line of vision and he followed its progress eagerly with his eyes, on to a gently fluttering leaf of a shrub oak growing in the hedgerow. Although common to the region, it was the first Broad-bodied Chaser that Stan had spotted so far this summer which quite made his day, even if not to the same extent as would another sighting of the blue moth. When he looked back along the road less than ten seconds later, following the flight path of the dragonfly, both the girl and the car had disappeared.

Any notion that there might have been something equally not quite right about this never occurred to Stan: the truth was, his attention was focused wholly on the dragonfly as it flitted from leaf to leaf. He never gave either the girl or the car and its driver another thought. Not then, that is.

Chapter Twelve

Cheryl was furious. She faced her fiancé in the short hallway of their flat as he came through the front door shortly before 6.30 p.m. that evening, barely giving him time to close it behind him. 'There's something seriously wrong with that girl,' she stormed at him. 'She made an absolute fool of me this afternoon. I didn't know where to put my face.'

Barry had had a difficult day. He was a laboratory technician employed at the town's main general hospital, still very much a trainee, and the paperwork relating to one of the cultures he'd been working on had gone missing which meant days of work had to be done all over again. This was not the welcome home he would have liked to find waiting for him. He couldn't believe the change in Cheryl since his mother's death, and he wasn't too sure how he felt about it. He looked at her wearily; would have liked to tell her that she was behaving like a fool at that moment, but anything for a quiet life.

'I take it you mean Linda,' he said.

'Of course I mean Linda!' she snapped. 'She was supposed to be there at your mother's house when I brought some more prospective clients over to view the property this afternoon. I told her when we'd be there and she promised me faithfully she wouldn't let me down.'

'So? You've got a key to the place, haven't you? Where's the problem? You're the sales negotiator, not Linda.' He suddenly noticed that she was wearing his mother's ring – she'd obviously collected it from the jewellers that day – and he felt a little annoyed that she hadn't spoken to him about this first and then let him check with Linda that she was OK about it.

'The front door was bolted, that was the problem, Barry,' snarled Cheryl, 'and the only key I have at the office is the one for that door!'

Cheryl's face darkened perceptibly. 'That girl is not right in the head, Barry. She'd locked and bolted the front door and then gone out by the kitchen door, locking that behind her as she went. You're going to have to do something: I'm seriously concerned about the way she's been behaving lately, all moody and secretive. You probably weren't listening, but I told you that when I showed those other people over the house the other day, I could smell Roy Adams's aftershave in the living-room. He'd been that day – I don't care what *you* say, I *wasn't* imagining it! – and if you want to know what I think, she's been with him again today.'

Barry looked at her. He could scarcely believe his ears. The suggestion was ludicrous: Linda felt as he did about Roy Adams; she couldn't stand the sight of the man and Cheryl knew it.

'And you needn't look at me like that, Barry!' Cheryl warned him. 'Roy Adams is grooming Linda to take your mother's place and help him to keep up the pressure on me to tell them, *him*, what he wants to hear.'

Barry sighed, dropping his car keys in a small bowl on the hall table. 'Then he's in for a big disappointment, isn't he? You can't tell him what isn't there for you to tell, can you?'

'He's never going to let go, Barry, and now that your mother's gone, he'll focus all of his attention on Linda. He's got to save face somehow, and if he doesn't get what he wants – a confession out of me for something I didn't do – he'll find some way of framing me. He's not going to give up after all this time, is he? He's determined to make the police look stupid.'

Barry looked at her for a moment. 'You know you're beginning to sound like Mum, don't you?'

'What do you mean?' she demanded.

'You're becoming as fixated about the whole business as they are – were, in Mum's case. Let it rest, Cheryl. The police know you're innocent.'

'No, Barry.' She shook her head adamantly. 'That's just it. They don't know anything of the sort. They simply didn't have enough evidence to make a case against me.'

He gave his head a slow shake.

'Don't you dare shake your head at me like that,' she warned him.

'Sorry,' he said. 'Seriously, Cheryl: what use could Linda be to Adams? She was a kid – barely six years old – when the accident happened; she knows nothing about it. I've never discussed it – your involvement in it – with her and neither did Mum. Linda's never shown the slightest interest in it: she lives in her own little dream world, you know that. You're letting your imagination run riot. The truth is – if only you'd face it – Linda couldn't care less about it. What's more, she hates Adams's guts even more than I do for what he did to Mum.'

'Then where is she, and why is he coming round all of a sudden to see her? I've phoned her half-a-dozen times since I've come in, both on her mobile and at home, and there's no answer. Maybe she's with that Eddie. What's his phone number?'

'Don't ask me,' replied Barry with a shrug. 'The most I know about him is that his name is Eddie. I've never met him, I don't think Mum had, either. I know Linda doesn't have a lot to say at the best of times, but I think we'd have picked up a clue here and there if he was someone special. He's just a guy she met and sees occasionally, probably while hanging out with a group of her friends.'

'But you do know where he lives, don't you?'

'No, I don't, and even if I did, I wouldn't go round to his place looking for her.' Barry looked at Cheryl crossly. 'Linda's perfectly entitled to come and go as she pleases. She's not a child.'

'That's where you're wrong, Barry,' said Cheryl darkly. 'She *is* a child, she'll be putty in Roy Adams's hands, and if you don't do something quickly about the way she's behaving, we're all going to be sorry.'

'OK, I'll speak to her,' he said with a faint sigh.

'*If* she comes home.'

'What's that supposed to mean?'

'I've told you: she's been strange, secretive, ever since your mother died.'

'I haven't noticed anything different about her.'

'Well, look again!' she snapped.

She turned away from Barry and, as she did so, an icy calm settled over her.

This isn't going to happen, she vowed to herself. *No one – Linda, that arrogant loser, Adams – is going to stand in my way. Not after all I've had to go through and do to get this far; not now that I'm so close to getting what I've schemed and plotted for all these years. Barry isn't going to do anything. Barry's a bit like those cultures he works on, basically stagnant and perfectly content to let everybody else get their hands dirty while all he has to do is sit tight and await positive developments. Well, watch this space!*

Chapter Thirteen

MRS CHARLES ROSE TO HER FEET AS THE MATRON OF THE WESTWAY Retirement Home crossed Reception to speak to her.

The matron gave her a regretful look. 'I am so sorry, Mrs Charles, but I am going to have to ask you to call on Mr Hendricks some other time. He's being rather naughty today and is refusing to see anybody.'

'Perhaps, if you would be kind enough to mention the name Cyril Forbes, Mr Hendricks might have a rethink,' suggested Mrs Charles.

The matron sighed a little. 'I'll give it a try, but I really feel it would be better if you came back another day.'

She walked away briskly, reappearing a few minutes later, giving Mrs Charles a quick nod and indicating to her to follow her.

Ronald Hendricks scowled at Mrs Charles as the matron ushered her into his room. He was sitting in a wheelchair in front of a large picture window that overlooked the rear of the home's grounds. A folded newspaper rested in his lap. The hands that gripped the arm-rests were cruelly twisted with arthritis which suggested to Mrs Charles that this might also be a problem with the rest of his body. 'You're not Cyril Forbes,' he growled, reinforcing his visitor's assumption concerning his overall physical condition as he shifted slightly in his chair and winced in pain.

'No,' she replied, stooping to retrieve the newspaper which had slipped to the floor from his lap. 'I am his elder sister, Adele.'

'Never knew he had a sister,' he said, eyeing her up and down disdainfully. 'Finally found one of those aliens he was always keeping an eye out for and taken off with it, has he? Never could understand the man's fascination with the little green men. Didn't seem quite normal to me. Brilliant children's performer, though; I'll give him that. Second to none.'

'Cyril's fine,' she said. 'Just as interested in outer space – and as you've said, little alien green men,' she put in with a small smile, 'and always will be.'

'Then why are you here pretending to be him?'

'I wanted to ask you about a children's party booking you passed on to him some years ago. You may remember—'

He cut in irritably. 'Not my fault it ended up a shambles. Got paid for his trouble, didn't he?'

'Yes, of course, he did,' she replied quickly. 'That isn't why I'm here. Cyril seemed to think that you might have been a friend of the family who were holding the party for their child.'

'Well, if I am, I've not noticed any of them troubling themselves to come and visit me here,' he said in a bitter voice.

'I'm sorry about that,' she said. She replaced the newspaper on his lap. 'And very sorry for bothering you: but thank you for seeing me.'

She turned to leave.

'Don't be in such a rush,' he said. 'Haven't seen an intelligent face worth the time and trouble of talking to ever since my son so very kindly arranged for my incarceration here. Bloody nurses – kids most of them – treat me like an infant! Matron's not much better. Talks down to me all the time. Drives me mad. Take a pew.' He waved a hand at the chair standing alongside his bed. 'Tell me what you find so interesting about that booking that's made you come all this way from – Little Gidding, isn't it? – to see a very grumpy old man.'

Mrs Charles collected the chair from the bedside and brought it nearer to him. Something told her that in addition to his arthritis, he would also be hard of hearing.

'I was hoping you could tell me something of the family and what was behind the cancellation of the booking.'

'You mean all the floral tributes and the hearse that suddenly rolled up? What a to-do, eh? They – the police – never found out for sure who was behind all that, you know. They checked with the florists in the town and drew a complete blank so far as knowing the identity of whoever had ordered the flowers. And as for the hearse ... that was stolen overnight from a local under-taker's. They never caught the culprit there, either. Strange business. Got my own thoughts on the matter, though. My late wife worked with the mother of the party girl ... in Templetons – that small department store in town. She told my wife it was because of that accidental death—' He broke off. 'Maybe you don't know about that.... Happened a few years before the party; got a lot of publicity at the time. The papers were full of it for days. Mrs Baxter – the party girl's mother – believed it was a vicious attempt to make her life a misery and I'd say she was probably right.'

'What did Mrs Baxter have to do with this accidental death?'

'Nothing. At least, only indirectly. You get *The Sketch* in your neck of the woods, don't you? Surely you read about this.'

'I was holidaying with friends in Italy at the time. In fact, Cyril has only just mentioned the birthday party to me. I understood from him that it was for a very young child.'

'It was. One of those chances in probably a million.... The Baxters had – have, so far as I am aware – two daughters, both born on the same day but quite a few years apart ... or so I was given to understand. Mrs Baxter told my wife it was the older daughter that the flowers and the hearse were meant for as some sort of twisted reminder of the accidental death the girl had got herself mixed up in. Ruined the day for everybody, including your brother.'

'Do you know if Mrs Baxter ever discussed the accidental death with your wife?'

He gave his head a quick shake. 'She might have at some point, but I doubt it. I seem to remember my wife feeling rather embar-rassed about the whole thing. I do know that she thought Mrs Baxter's daughter was as guilty as the very devil – everybody did – and that she avoided making any mention of the accident in case Mrs Baxter caught on to how she felt. They had to work together; the last thing my wife wanted was bad feeling between them. It was one of those strange … well, tragedies, if you like. Maybe it was an accident, maybe it wasn't. Who knows? It all happened a good while ago now, as I've said, but at the time, there wouldn't have been too many local Gidding people who didn't feel that there was something not quite right about the whole business. Just a feeling everyone had, and bad luck for the girl concerned – the one they believed wasn't as innocent as she pretended – if everything was as the witnesses claimed and it was a straightforward accident. She's probably lived it down now, though. But it must have been a bit rough for her for a time there.'

Mrs Charles looked at him thoughtfully. 'Wouldn't it be reasonable to think that it was the mother of the dead girl who sent the flowers and arranged for someone to steal the hearse?'

'Very reasonable,' he agreed. 'Except for one thing: she was dead; had a history of mental problems and died not long after the accident that claimed her daughter's life. Not surprisingly, this – the mother's death – stirred up a lot more publicity and speculation about the accident, and I particularly remember my wife saying that in her opinion, the woman had died of a broken heart. If my memory serves me correctly – but please don't quote me on this – she was a single mother, struggling on her own to raise her daughter.'

He paused and looked at Mrs Charles curiously. 'You're very interested in something that's been confined to the department of hopeless causes all these years.'

She agreed. 'I have reason to believe that I've been consulted by one of the children invited to the party you asked Cyril to take on for you. She's been suffering from a particularly distressing recurring dream over what happened that day, and I had hoped you would be able to shed some light on the matter for me so that I can help her.'

'Not a bloody psychiatrist, are you?'

'No,' she said quietly. 'I'm a clairvoyant.'

'Good God!' he exclaimed.

'If only,' she responded with a grave smile.

Chapter fourteen

Roy Adams's car swept on to the driveway of his home, originally a farmhouse and riding stables, the latter located in substantial outbuildings and his reason, initially, for buying the property. The stables were ripe for conversion and in which case, would prove to be a good investment for the future.

He felt reasonably pleased with himself. They had been cagey at the Little Gidding Post Office Stores when he had called there, pretending to be looking to buy a bungalow in the area and enquiring as to whether the owner of the pretty little one he had passed on his way into the village, would consider selling, but he had basically got what he was really looking for. The bungalow was owned by a Mrs Edwina Charles, a clairvoyant: this was as much as the villagers to whom he had spoken were prepared to tell him. One elderly woman, obviously notorious in the village for her talkativeness, had been shot clear warnings in the form of stony stares when she had showed signs of wanting to be a little too helpful to a complete stranger.

It was enough; all Roy needed to know. Linda was holding out about something, and being the silly, airheaded little ditherer she was, she'd consulted a clairvoyant to tell her what to do. He didn't question her knowing the clairvoyant well enough to seek her out: assumed that she had got to know the woman a few years earlier when she had done some summer work for a local farmer.

He decided to make himself a cup of tea, and then he would challenge her about what he had discovered. If she were a very good girl and told him what he wanted to know, now that he had this further information about the woman she had called on

54

yesterday, he would let her go. He was determined to get to the bottom of this clairvoyant business, if it was the last thing he did!

After promising her a lift home from Little Gidding the previous afternoon, with, as he had put it to her, "no funny business", he had carried on instead to his own home, as he had always intended, with her as his hostage until she told him what she was doing in the village. She'd said that she was looking for some summer work again, but he knew that was a lie. He had permitted her to sleep in the house overnight – a rare privilege: Roy didn't like anyone other than himself inside his home, or using any of its conveniences, and had actually been waiting outside the bathroom door with a bucket filled with an assortment of cleaning utensils after Linda had finished in there that morning.

He had taken her out to the stables, shutting her inside an old horse box kept round the back of the stabling and left there by the previous owner of the property, while he had carried out his undercover investigations in Little Gidding; hadn't wanted to risk his nearest neighbour, who was always round threatening him with what he would do if he didn't stop shooting birds and making all that racket late every afternoon with his shotgun. Roy was confident that Linda wouldn't plead for help from his neighbour and say she had been taken hostage: he was rather more concerned that his neighbour would spread tittle-tattle about the young woman he had encountered (perhaps) in his home.

Linda was told that the horse box wasn't locked, she was free to leave at anytime she chose; warned that if she didn't wait for his return, she had a good twelve-mile-walk ahead of her back into town, and on a very hot summer's day. He knew she'd stay put. A young girl wandering along seldom used country lanes, looking for a ride into town, could arouse suspicions: questions could well be asked, questions Linda wouldn't want to answer. He also knew she wouldn't phone anyone for help. The beautiful thing about Linda was that she was even more scared of stirring up old demons than she was of him.

Roy's garage was some distance from the house, down a sloping drive of loose chippings that was flanked on either side by a wide expanse of regularly cut grass and finished at a tree-bordered stream. He garaged his car and, as he turned to leave, wiped a smudge of dust off the bonnet with the duster he kept on a shelf for that precise purpose. He then headed back to the house, scowling into the distance at the sign advertising the local firm that had supplied and installed new UPVC replacement windows and doors to his property, and with whose managing director, as was Roy's wont, he was currently in dispute.

Someone was sitting in his large, high-back wicker chair on the patio. The chair was turned slightly away from him: he couldn't see the whole person, whether it was a he or a she, only the slim, blue-jeaned, casually crossed leg that kept swinging out rhymically.

It wasn't his neighbour determinedly waiting for his return, as had happened on more than one occasion in the past. His neighbour was in his eighties, had legs on him like tree trunks, and furthermore, at his age, wouldn't be seen dead in jeans.

Roy leapt the six steps up to his patio, two at a time, ready to do battle at this unwanted intrusion. He didn't get a chance to say a word, though: through his inability to control his rising ire, he missed his footing on the last of the steps and when he recovered himself, found himself looking up both barrels of his own shotgun.

Chapter Fifteen

THE LOUD REPORT FROM THE SHOTGUN MADE LINDA'S BLOOD RUN cold. Roy Adams was back – she knew that; she'd heard his car on the drive – and now he was out there on his patio shooting birds. He'd probably seen how upset it had made her as a child to see this mindless slaughter and now he was using it to unsettle her and force her to tell him what he wanted to know.

She was sitting on an old, three-legged milking stool, clutching her shoulder bag in her lap, as if fearful someone was standing over her and threatening to snatch it from her. She was frozen in this position for almost ten minutes while she waited for the sickening sound of more shooting, but everything had gone deathly quiet. Roy had gone inside, she finally decided, getting up off the stool and then pushing open the door of the horse box.

Slinging the strap of her bag over one shoulder, she walked slowly round the back of the stables and then started up to the house which was some fifty yards distant. It was a moment or two before she saw Roy, and a further moment or two before she made some sort of sense of what she was seeing. He was lying flat on his back, arms and legs splayed wide; as if, she thought, he had been climbing the steps up to the patio and had lost his balance and fallen backwards down them.

He wasn't moving and she expected to find that he had struck his head on the ground and knocked himself senseless.

She couldn't begin to think what she would do if she were right. She had her mobile with her; she could phone for help, call an ambulance. But then because of who he was and who she was

and their past relationship through her mother, questions would
be asked; questions she didn't want asked and didn't want to
answer.

She felt cornered. One way or another, it really was all going to
start again, wasn't it? She had prayed as she had never prayed
before that it had ended with her mother's death. But it hadn't; it
wasn't going to, she could see that now. Roy Adams was going to
get his own way, she thought desperately.

The shotgun she assumed he had been using was clearly visible,
lying horizontally across his chest.

Her steps slowed dramatically as she neared him.

She was still some distance from him, but she could nevertheless see that there was something resembling a huge red ink-blot
that had spread wide across the front of his pale-blue pilot's shirt
and down to the belted waistband on his slacks.

He'd shot himself in the chest, that was her first thought –
accidentally, of course – as he had fallen from the patio.

She came to a stop and watched his chest for several moments
to see if it would rise and fall; if he were still alive.

Her eyes watered with strain; she couldn't be sure of what she
was seeing. One minute she was positive he was still breathing,
the next convinced that he was dead.

She turned away, towards the drive and then, lowering her
head, started down it to the road. She hadn't told anybody she
was there, and she knew he hadn't: she should get away from
there as fast as possible.

But what if he were still alive? a little voice at the back of her
head whispered. *Do you want that on your conscience for the rest
of your life; that you deliberately let him die?* And what if it
somehow came out that she'd been there that day at his home?
What if someone had seen her there? It would look very suspicious if she didn't do something to help him, wouldn't it? The
police wouldn't have to look far to find witnesses who would
swear she hated Roy Adams.

She had to go back and be sure.

She walked on tiptoe up to him, almost as if afraid he'd hear
her coming and suddenly sit up and say something challenging to

her, or admit that it was a joke he was playing on her, and then laugh at her for being such a baby.

He didn't move.

What if he was doing this to scare her? she asked herself. He might think that if he scared her in this way, she'd finally talk to him. That would be typical of Roy Adams.

She came as near as she dared to him, reaching out sideways with a tentative hand to snatch up the shotgun. Just in case he was thinking of springing up and turning it on her to frighten her, she told herself.

She stepped well back from him – this was in case her worst fears were confirmed and he suddenly sprang up and made a grab for her. For as long as she could remember, her mother and brother had always treated her as if she were one or twopence short of a pound, in effect brainwashing her to accept this as a truism. For once, though, she thought that what she was thinking was quite intelligent. She had looked round at the patio steps and could see that if Roy had stumbled and fallen backwards with the shotgun in his hands, it would not be lying neatly across his chest as she had found it. A more likely place to see it would be on the steps themselves, or down on one side of them.

She carefully put the shotgun down on the ground and started to back away from it, as if she had touched something that she now knew was contaminated with a deadly virus.

Roy Adams was dead. Somebody had deliberately shot him with his own shotgun and then placed it across his body. And now she'd handled the murder weapon. Her fingerprints would be on it.

Her brother would go mad at her for being so stupid. Cheryl would never let her forget it.

If she told them….

Chapter Sixteen

'I CAN'T SAY CLIVE MERTON WAS TOO THRILLED ABOUT MY INTEREST in Jo Sowerby's death, but' – David Sayer smiled to himself as he recalled his means of getting what he had wanted from Merton – 'he came good in the finish.'

He paused and looked at Edwina Charles thoughtfully. 'Both Clive and the senior detective who looked into her death were, and remain, perfectly satisfied with the overall findings. The cause of death was cardiac arrest which, so far as Clive is concerned, will stand. I asked him to look at the whole picture – specifically the accidental drowning at the gravel pit that set the woman off on her persistent campaign to uncover what she believed to be the true story of what really happened that day – and while I'm not going to agree with you, or the late Jo Sowerby, for that matter, that the whole story never came out, I have to admit to feeling a little uneasy after Clive got back to me. I can't tell you why; the best I can come up with is that something of the way you think is beginning to rub off on me. And I don't mean I'm turning into a clairvoyant!'

Mrs Charles smiled. 'Was there more than one thing that Mr Merton told you that made you feel this way, or one thing in particular?'

Trust her, David thought, *to go for the jugular!*

He was quiet for a moment. Then he said, 'There were six of them at the gravel pit that day. Four boys and two girls ... the girl who drowned in the gravel pit – her name was Valerie Ward – and Cheryl Baxter. All four boys made similar statements, confirming that Cheryl had left them to go after Valerie, who, as I've told you, had gone off home in a huff over some petty quarrel with Cheryl.'

'Do you know the names of the boys?'

He nodded. 'Barry Kellar, Cheryl Baxter's present fiancé, Andrew Tomlinson – he emigrated to New Zealand with his family the following year and there's no record of the family ever having returned to the UK – and Jonathon Lewis. Merton doesn't know what became of him, but I've checked and there's no Lewis family living in Gidding or its environs, so he moved away with his family at some point, too.'

'The fourth boy?'

David frowned a little. 'This is where I began to feel a little uneasy.... The fourth boy in the group committed suicide less than three months later: he was found at the gravel pit, hanging by the neck from one of the trees there. His name was Bernard Watson. There were no suspicious circumstances, according to Clive. There was some suggestion of bullying at school – it seems he was one if these sensitive kids, easily upset – but if this were the case, the culprit or culprits were never apprehended. Clive said there was a code of silence in regard to the bullying that the investigating police officers tried to break and failed; and besides, discovering who the bullies were wasn't going to bring the lad back, was it? The school's head was taken to one side and advised to make sure his staff kept a close eye on this sort of thing and stamped it out before it got out of hand, and that was it. The verdict of the coroner at the inquest was suicide. Case closed.'

He looked at the clairvoyant. 'Well, has that satisfied these funny feelings of yours?'

She was quiet for a moment. Then, with a small shake of her head, she said, 'I'm afraid not. If anything, they are stronger and grow stronger by the day. Jo Sowerby's gift of a tarot reading was finally claimed yesterday, not by the intended recipient, but by her daughter, Linda, who had reason for believing that the gift was for her. However, before I did the reading, she told me of a recurring dream she was having.'

Mrs Charles paused, averting her gaze from David and then pensively concentrating it on the middle distance. He thought she looked worried which didn't do a lot for the unease he had been experiencing since talking to Clive Merton. At length coming back to David, she went on, 'My impression was that once Linda found herself with no means of escape, so to speak, the dream was the tactic she employed to divert me from uncovering what really troubled her. The reverse proved to be the case. In telling me of her dream, Linda gave me the key I needed to begin to unlock the truth, the real reason why she came to me for a reading.'

Dear me, thought David. *Here we go again, off into the realms of fantasy. Merton would love this!*

Mrs Charles read the expression on his face. 'It wasn't just a dream, Superintendent. It was something that really happened when she was a child.'

'The cards told you this?'

'No, Cyril, my brother.' She smiled to herself. She knew exactly what David Sayer thought of Cyril Forbes and what Cyril Forbes thought of David Sayer who, in the past, as a senior police officer, had been charged on one occasion with moving Cyril on when he was going through his Gidding placard-waving days, warning of what he termed, "the coming".

She then went on to explain how her brother came to see the floral tributes and hearse that Linda saw repeatedly in her dream. 'Cyril said the police were also in attendance,' she continued. 'Somebody had obviously sent for them. Unfortunately, Cyril has no idea what it was all about, but from what I've been able to gather, both from his version of the events of that afternoon and from speaking to the retired magician who passed the booking on to him, I would find it very difficult to believe that an unfortunate mistake had been made by someone. The hearse and flowers arrived at their intended destination.'

'Some kids' party that must have been,' David remarked.

'Quite terrifying, I would have said. It certainly was from Linda's point of view. She's had nightmares about it ever since.'

'When did this happen?'

'The birthday girl was nine or ten – Cyril isn't sure, that sort of thing doesn't register with him – and so Linda would have been around the same age which means this happened roughly seven years ago.'

David nodded. 'And you'd like to know what the flowers and hearse were all about…. Clive will be charmed, I'm sure!'

She smiled. 'I know what it was all about, it was there in Linda's tarot reading: I am merely curious to hear the official police version of events.'

He looked at her for a moment. 'What was in the reading?'

'Nothing good, Superintendent.'

Chapter Seventeen

Edwina Charles was hesitant as she dealt out the eleven cards in the small pack of tarot cards that she had placed to one side after Linda had left the previous afternoon.

'This places me in a rather awkward position,' she said after a moment. 'In the past, my explanations to you of a reading I have given have, as a rule, related to those who have consulted me and have then later died in suspicious circumstances. Technically speaking, the disclosure of any aspect of Linda's reading is in serious breach of my obligation to observe client confidentiality. She is also very young....'

David, looking at the cards she had dealt out, nodded and said, 'It's all the more difficult to break their trust.'

'However,' the clairvoyant went on, 'in this instance, there are two reasons why I feel that I can justify my negation of this obligation. The first: the gift was not for Jo Sowerby's daughter, it was intended for her son's fiancée, Cheryl Baxter, and so it could be said that Linda was seeking a reading from me under false pretences, albeit unwittingly. My second reason for taking you into my confidence is that the cards have revealed to me that there is a serious threat to Linda's life which will inevitably come to pass if something isn't done swiftly to prevent this from happening.'

Mrs Charles had placed the tarot cards in two separate rows, one under the other, five in the first row and six in the second.

'It is a reading using a name spread,' she explained. 'The first five cards represent the seeker's first name, in this instance, Linda. She doesn't have a middle name, so the second row of six represents her surname, Kellar.'

'I don't see the death card in that little lot,' David remarked.

'Don't you?' she said mildly. She pointed to the first card in the spread, one from the Major Arcana, Card number IV, *L'Empereur*, or *The Emperor*.

'It's upside-down,' David observed.

'Reversed,' she corrected him. 'This card reveals Linda's immaturity and basically weak character. The next card, *Le Chariot – The Chariot* – again from the Major Arcana and again reversed, indicates a persistent unwillingness to accept full responsibility for her life and actions, and an ingrained inability to face reality. The third card, this one from the Minor Arcana, *Chevalier Des Épées*, or *The Cavalier of Swords*, reinforces the one immediately before it, *The Chariot*. The fourth card is my old friend' – she smiled wryly – '*La Maison De Dieu*, or *The Lightning Struck Tower*, which is also reversed. This card tells me that this young, rather foolish but likeable girl is at serious risk of finding herself entrapped.'

'What do you mean? Somebody's going to kidnap her – hold her against her will?'

'Yes and no. She will willingly walk into the trap that has been laid for her; won't even see it as such. Someone is soon to use her for their own ends – that is, if that person hasn't already done so, and this is where the danger to her life will arise. The last card in the first row, an unnumbered card from the Major Arcana, *Le Mat – The Fool* – again points to her immaturity and inability, or reluctance, to make the right choices in life. She will make the wrong choice here in her willingness to be used and entrapped. Those five cards relate very positively to this girl in her past and immediate situation. She is what she is, and more than likely will remain so, leaning on others wherever possible, and letting them make all of the decisions concerning her life. However, in her defence, I firmly believe that these detrimental traits in her character stem from a lack of self-belief which I also believe, when relating my reading to her dream, can be laid firmly at her mother's doorstep. Linda has never been given a true opportunity to express herself and be the person she would have been had her family influences been different. She reminds me of one of the

PH

jurors in *Alice in Wonderland*. She has been suppressed all her life and sat upon.'

'Well, yes, I can agree with that,' he said with a nod. 'Alcoholics are notoriously quick to put people down: it can't have been a picnic living with Jo Sowerby.'

'*The Cavalier of Swords* indicates that the threat to her life will definitely come from a man, somebody she has in the past, or will in the future, put her trust in without question.'

Mrs Charles then pointed to the first card in the second row, *The Cavalier of Cups*.

'Reversed,' David noted.

'Which reinforces the destructive influence some man has or will have over her,' Mrs Charles explained. 'A man who is both sly and cunning – extremely clever, in fact. A man to whom artifice and trickery come naturally.'

She was momentarily thoughtful; gazed at the cards for some moments before speaking again. Then, pointing to the next card, *The Five of Deniers* or *Diamonds*, she said, 'All of the foregoing relates to this one card from the Minor Arcana. Linda has done something extremely silly, made a very serious error of judgement, which is not terribly surprising, bearing in mind her character traits – this inability and unwillingness of hers to face reality, and her natural inclination to shy away from dealing in a responsible fashion with anything that she feels will disrupt her life. The next card, *The Queen of Swords*, represents her mother, and it is here that Linda's error of judgement will ultimately result in a threat to her life.'

Mrs Charles paused and gazed thoughtfully across the room before turning her head to look directly at David. 'Linda is concealing something, Superintendent ... something concerning her mother that she has decided is best concealed for fear that it would otherwise seriously disrupt her life and the lives of those closest to her, her brother and his fiancée. Unfortunately for Linda, this concealment will achieve the exact opposite, the very thing she fears.'

Mrs Charles looked away and was quiet for a moment. 'Linda was afraid of her mother, I am quite sure of this, and I am equally sure that the woman she hears laughing in her dream is her mother.'

'Her mother is laughing at her?'

'No, if anything, her mother should have been angry with her for the way she behaved when told that the birthday party was over – there would be no magician, no Punch and Judy show, and that everybody had to pack up and go home. In her dream, she starts to scream: my brother can confirm that this is actually exactly what happened on the day. The children were screaming, Linda, he seems to think, loudest of all.'

'So what do you think her mother found so funny?'

'I think Jo Sowerby was laughing at the Baxter family's reaction to the floral tributes and the hearse that had turned up. Moreover, I think Linda subconsciously knows this and that not impossibly, she knows instinctively why her mother found it all so amusing. This is what she really finds so terrifying about her dream.'

'Well, the poor woman was always three sheets to the wind. All sense of decency and decorum would have evaporated once she was in her cups. From what I've heard said of the woman, I doubt that she was ever completely sober.'

'A truly unpleasant story begins to unfold with this card, *The Moon*,' said Mrs Charles, pointing to it. 'Particularly when read in conjunction with the previous card, *The Queen of Swords*, representing Linda's mother. The crayfish you see at the bottom of *The Moon*, and which I am sure I have described to you before, is symbolical of that which derives from the deep and unknown, and points directly at something or someone unsuspected. In all probability, both. *Something and someone unsuspected*,' the clairvoyant reiterated grimly. 'And, as I have said, *The Moon's* reinforcement of *The Queen of Swords*, the mother card, indicates to me a distinct possibility that Jo Sowerby was behind the dispatch of the flowers and hearse to the Baxter home on the day of the birthday party.'

'I don't get it. Why would she do something like that?'

'As a malicious threat, perhaps, to the Baxter family for protecting their elder daughter, Cheryl, who was guilty of murder.

In Jo Sowerby's eyes, that is. The next card, *The Eight of Swords*, indicates the domination that Linda has experienced in the past and will continue to experience in the future if no effort is made to alter what is to come. The final card, *The Sun*, reversed, suggests that there will be no such effort made. Linda must simply change the pattern of her life in order to disperse the serious cloud that I see hanging over her life. She must make amends, make right this silly mistake she's made.'

There was a small silence. Then David said, 'Are you sure you haven't been overly influenced by your visit from Jo Sowerby?'

'And allowed my imagination to run away with me along the same lines as hers?' Mrs Charles smiled. 'No, Superintendent. I've thought and said it all along: there is something terribly wrong here.'

She was silent for a moment. 'The question to be asked and answered is the one you raised a moment or two ago. *Why would she do something like that?* Why was Jo Sowerby so obsessively convinced that the truth had not come out about the gravel-pit girl's death, and why did she make it her personal crusade throughout the years that have passed since this tragedy, to bring what she believed to be the truth, to light?'

'It's not something Merton hasn't thought about,' David confessed. 'But nobody knows.'

'Or bothered to find out.'

He nodded his agreement. 'I'm not making excuses, but I think it's understandable that the police weren't interested in listening to the ramblings of a woman who was already known to them for being a heavy drinker and a committed troublemaker.'

He hesitated. Then he said, 'If it's not an impertinent question, how much of your reading did you tell Linda?'

'Nothing of its more sinister aspects. The only definite warning I gave her was to be on her guard and to choose her friends wisely. I also advised her to sit down and think very carefully about what will become of her if she carries on as she is at present and continues to be so indecisive about everything that touches her. I pointed out that she was letting life drift past her and away, out of her reach, and that she must grab it by the horns; decide what she wants for the future and act upon it swiftly, now, before it is too late.'

'You didn't mention this mysterious error of judgement of hers?'

'No. I have asked her to think over what I have told her and then come back to me, say in a week or two's time. Her life hangs by a slender thread on this mistake she has made and I couldn't risk panicking her into doing something even more foolish which, I feel, is a distinct possibility. She left with no idea that I was fully aware that she was concealing something, and not just from me, from everyone.'

'What did she have to say about all of this?'

'Very little. She wanted somebody to step in and take control, she hoped that person would be me, and my impression was that she left here yesterday totally unimpressed with my unwillingness to bow to her needs and give her a day by day clear directive on how she should live her life. In fact, if you think about it, there was nothing that I told her that her mother and, in all probability, her brother, haven't said to her a thousand times.'

'You're not going to leave this alone, are you?'

'I can't,' she replied. She looked directly at him. 'Can I?'

Chapter Eighteen

DULL COLOUR CREPT UP LINDA'S FACE AS SHE WAITED FOR SOMEONE to answer the front door of Eddie Nuttall's nan's home. She didn't know his nan's name. She had looked up Nuttall in the phone book the other day, just for something to do, but no one of that name was living at this address which could only mean that his grandmother was related to him on his mother's side.

Linda didn't make many decisions in regard to what she should or should not do, but of those she had made, this one had been the hardest by a long shot on which to act positively. She desperately needed help, somewhere to stay until…. She couldn't think that far, didn't want to think that far, just prayed somebody would find Roy Adams's body and call the police, and that it would all blow over quickly so she could go home.

As she waited, the first of those agonizingly familiar *what ifs* crept into her mind. What if Eddie weren't there and his nan answered the door? What was she going to say to her? Did his nan know anything about her? Of course not. She'd only been out with Eddie twice, which wasn't strictly true as they'd been with a group of other young people both times and had only just sort of drifted into one another's company as each of those evenings had worn on. He'd told her that he worked three nights a week as a shelf filler at a supermarket – she didn't know which one, she hadn't thought to ask – and that if it hadn't been for his virtually bedridden nan, who was apparently his only close relative, he would have gone on to university. He had planned on a career in journalism; had hoped to obtain degrees in English literature and sociology. That was all she knew about him. She thought they were about the same age as one another; hadn't liked to ask.

The door finally opened and Eddie Nuttall stood before her, tucking a clean white shirt into the waistband of what looked to be freshly ironed jeans. He looked different away from the glaringly bright lights of the clubs where they would meet. A lot older, much more mature. But maybe that had something to do with his having to look after an elderly relative. She remembered her mother once remarking that constant close contact with the elderly was a sure-fire means of a carer ageing ahead of time and definitely not for her.

'Oh,' said Linda. 'You're going out....'

Eddie gave himself a moment to take in her general appearance. Her face was damp with perspiration; there were dark circles under her eyes and the hand she used to brush back the thick strands of hair that flopped down low over her forehead, was trembling slightly. 'No,' he said. 'It's OK. Nan's arthritis has been giving her gyp today. She's just chucked a cup of tea over me. I've had to change out of my wet things.'

'Oh,' she said.

They looked at one another.

'Do you want to come in?' he asked after a moment. He spoke casually. No one would have guessed how taken aback he was by her visit. It was the last thing he would have expected a little mouse like Linda Kellar to do.

'I—' Linda knit her brow. 'What about your nan?'

'She's upstairs doing her needlepoint. She hardly ever comes downstairs these days; the stairs have got too much for her. She's got everything she needs, her telly and her precious soaps, up in her room. It'll be all right.' He saw a look of hesitancy come into Linda's eyes, a hint that she might have been about to take flight. 'She's not dangerous, she won't bite you. I shouldn't have said that about the tea. She didn't really chuck it over me. She lost her balance as she moved to take her lunch tray from me and knocked it out of my hands.'

Linda thought for a moment, then nodded and, as he moved to one side, stepped through the doorway into the hall. He saw her look up at the ceiling, as if listening for sounds up there, and then look anxiously at the stairs, as if expecting to see someone come rushing down at her like Norman Bates in *Psycho*, dressed as Bates's mother and brandishing a knife. She really was a strange one, he thought.

'You won't hear a peep out of her: the needlepoint only gets noisy when she gets really worked up and overexcited about something,' he said in a dry voice.

Linda looked at him quickly, but said nothing.

He noticed that she was limping, keeping her right heel well up from making contact with the carpet. 'What have you done to your foot?' he asked.

'I've got a blister on my heel. My shoe hurts.' She had walked five wearying long miles since leaving Roy Adams's place, sometimes crossing fields to avoid being seen, before successfully hailing a hopper bus on the outskirts of Gidding and getting a ride the rest of the way into the town centre. Her whole body was aching with exhaustion and tension.

'How did you know where to find me?' he asked her curiously, taking her through to the living-room.

'You told me – I mean,' she added quickly, seeing the odd look that came suddenly into his eyes, 'you said your nan's house backed on to the railway.'

'There are miles of railway running through Gidding,' he pointed out. 'No wonder you're limping.'

She had willingly sat down on one end of the sofa that he had indicated and was focusing her gaze on a worn patch on the armrest, avoiding looking at him. *Somebody else who thinks I'm stupid*, she thought. Well, for once she agreed with him. She must have been out of her mind to come here! There wasn't any alternative, though, was there? If she'd gone home, Barry – no, Cheryl, Barry wouldn't have bothered – would've wanted to know where she'd been; wouldn't have let up on her. It would be all right after Roy Adams's body was found, she told herself.

'It was that time when I said I had to leave early to pick up my mum from the pub where she worked,' she said. 'You said your nan's home backed on to the railway that runs directly behind the pub. You also said something about being busy during the day rebuilding her front brick wall. You said it was beginning to collapse on to the footpath. I noticed – you're still working on it.'

He looked at her for a moment. Now there was a surprise. She was nowhere near as dim-witted as everyone thought. 'I didn't believe you that night … about your having to leave early to pick up your mother. You just said that, didn't you?'

'I thought – I thought you might be looking for an excuse to....'

'To do what? Get shut of you?'

'Something like that,' she admitted.

'You're a funny one, Linda,' he said. 'OK then, if you're so sure that I wanted to get shut of you, what are you doing here now?'

'I shouldn't have come.'

He flopped down in an armchair, long, slim legs stretched out, hands clasped behind his head. He waited.

'I'm in big trouble,' she said.

'Who with? Your brother?'

She shook her head, frowning a little. 'He's all right. He – he pretty much leaves me alone; lets me do what I want without making a fuss.'

'The lovely bride-to-be, then … Cheryl?'

Linda looked at him sharply. She had never told him that she had a brother, and nothing on earth would have made her want to mention Cheryl's name or anything about her to anyone. One of their mutual friends might have mentioned them to him, but why would they? None of them knew Barry and Cheryl. They were way out of their age group. 'How did you know that I have a brother?'

'I went to school, Linda: I can read. It was in the papers … when your mother died.' He paused for a moment, watching her face closely. She was jumpy, suspicious of him; would clam up and not tell him why she was there if he didn't watch himself.

'I can't go home,' she blurted out. 'I need somewhere to stay … just for a day or two, that's all.'

He looked at her searchingly. This was one complication he could well do without. 'Are you going to tell me what this is all about, or are we going to sit here for the rest of the day playing questions and answers?'

'It's my mother's' – she hesitated – 'her boyfriend.'

He eyed her thoughtfully. 'What about him?'

'He – he's been pestering me ever since my mother died, coming to my home when ... when he knows Barry and Cheryl won't be there and I'm all alone.'

'What do you mean? He's – what ... trying it on with you ... looking for sex? For God's sake, Linda, what on earth's the matter with you? Tell your brother,' he said when she made no reply. 'Let him sort it.'

'I can't....'

He waited for an explanation. When none was forthcoming, he said, 'Why not? Come on, Linda.' He spoke irritably. 'Out with it.'

'He – this man was behind a lot of my mother's troubles. Barry and I blame him for her drinking; he was a bad influence, and we thought we were free of him after she died. He's a really nasty man; Barry's no match for him. It wouldn't be fair of me to tell him what's been going on behind his back, not when he and Cheryl are so close to getting married. They've got too much else on their minds. This man' – Linda hesitated momentarily, frowning over what she should say next in reinforcement of her argument – 'he's the sort who would go out of his way to spoil their day, just for the fun of it. I'm sorry, I shouldn't have come.' Her cheeks were burning a bright red. 'What will your nan think? I – I didn't know where else to go....' Her voice tailed off.

'You've got friends – a girlfriend you could go and stay with for a bit, haven't you?'

'Barry knows all of my friends, where they live; that's the first place he'll go looking for me, but that won't be for a day or two – Barry isn't a worrier – and I'll be back home by then. This man hasn't actually done anything wrong, I wouldn't want him to get into any trouble; it's just that it's best I'm if not there, at home, when he calls round next time, and then maybe he'll get the message and leave me alone.'

'What if he doesn't?'

'I'll tell Barry.'

'You'd better,' he said. He looked at her thoughtfully. There

was a lot more bugging her than the alleged unwelcome atten-
tions of Roy Adams, and that was who she was talking about.
Lying, more like. Roy Adams hadn't pestered her for sex in the
past and wouldn't in the future. Nothing surer.

Chapter Nineteen

THE ATTRACTIVE, FAIR-HAIRED YOUNG WOMAN SITTING AT A SMALL table with Edwina Charles, drinking caffè latte in the town's busy shopping mall, said her name was Amelia Blankhert. She hadn't given a name yesterday when Mrs Charles had spoken to her on the phone, wanting to speak to Bernard Watson's mother and asking if she could call on her to discuss Valerie Ward's accident. In fact, Amelia had denied knowing anyone of that name, and when Mrs Charles had tried to explain why she was phoning, was brusquely told that she had approached the wrong family and had had the phone put down abruptly in her ear.

Amelia had immediately phoned the police and made a complaint.

'It was the police who told me who you are and where to find you,' she began by way of explanation for contacting the clair-voyant and agreeing to meet her in the mall that morning. 'I apologize for my rudeness yesterday, but I couldn't possibly agree to your talking to my mother. She was never the same after my brother's suicide; became suicidal herself when Jo Sowerby and a policeman by the name of Adams started pestering her for infor-mation about the circumstances surrounding Valerie's death. In the finish, my late father had to take out a court injunction against the two of them: they were not permitted to come within a hundred yards of my mother, or to have any contact with her whatsoever. I have agreed to see you now and tell you what little I know of that girl's death, but only on condition that I have your assurance that you will never try and contact my mother again.'

'You have my word,' said Mrs Charles, and thanked her. Then, after thoughtfully studying the young woman for a moment or two, 'You were some years older than your brother when he died,' she observed.

'Yes, I had just turned twenty-one. I got married the month before Bernard hanged himself and had moved with my husband, who is a Dutchman, to the Netherlands to live. I come home as often as I can to see my mother, and by and large, she is coping quite well now, far better than she has in years, and I am naturally anxious that nothing should upset her, and particularly anything that touches on my brother's suicide and Valerie Ward.'

'I take it she knows that Jo Sowerby is dead,' said Mrs Charles.

'Yes, and while it may seem a dreadful thing to say, that woman's death has lifted a great weight off her shoulders.'

Mrs Charles looked at her curiously. 'Are you saying that there was something your mother could have told Mrs Sowerby about Valerie Ward's accidental drowning?'

Amelia stirred her coffee, gazing thoughtfully into the swirling liquid.

'May I first ask what your interest is in Valerie's accident?' She raised her eyes to look directly at Mrs Charles. There was something guarded in them, a suggestion, thought the clairvoyant, that she hadn't quite made up her mind if meeting her like this was a mistake.

'I am beginning to share Jo Sowerby's conviction that there was more to it,' replied Mrs Charles, after deciding that the best way forward now was to be frank and open at the outset about her motives for discussing the accident.

A flash of irritation crossed Amelia's face. 'As a clairvoyant you have reached this conclusion? This is something you saw in a crystal ball, or was it your spirit contact who gave you this information?' She laughed coldly. 'Don't tell me that dreadful woman came to you for her answers? She really was getting desperate if she turned to a clairvoyant as her last resort.'

'Be that as it may,' Mrs Charles responded mildly, 'whatever really happened that day at the gravel pit, if I fail to uncover the truth—'

Amelia cut in sharply. 'And so it starts again. First Jo Sowerby and Roy Adams, and now you.'

'I have given you my word, I will not contact either you or your mother again.'

'I don't know how many times it has to be said! Nothing *really* happened, as you have put it, that day. It was a straightforward accident.'

'An accident that I suspect resulted in your brother taking his life,' Mrs Charles reminded her.

'Regrettably, yes.' Amelia paused to allow several shoppers to walk past their table and move out of earshot. She pressed a paper napkin to her lips; spent a moment or two contemplating the faint smear of lipstick on it. Then she said, 'Valerie was pregnant, at least this was what she told my brother. She said my brother was the father of the child and initially, there was no reason to doubt her word ... bearing in mind' she put in drily 'that my mother had come home early from work one day and found the pair of them in bed together, having sex. There was hell to pay, of course. There was Bernard talking about taking on the responsibilities of fatherhood and there they were, both barely fourteen years old, for goodness' sake! But' – Amelia sighed – 'my brother dug in his heels: he said he loved Valerie and wanted the child – he could see no reason why they couldn't play happy families together with their baby – and then when Valerie died, he wanted to die, too. And so he took his life which, with hindsight, I think, wasn't terribly surprising. Perhaps if our parents had handled the situation a little more delicately, Bernard might be alive today.'

'Was Valerie happy to go along with your brother's plans for them?'

Amelia dabbed at her mouth some more. 'I very much doubt it. My mother said it was all in his head. Valerie was a little scrubber. Or so my mother said. I didn't know the girl; I never laid eyes on her.'

'How much of this did Jo Sowerby know?'

'About the pregnancy? Nothing. My mother never mentioned a word about it to anyone – outside of our immediate family, I mean. Not even after my brother's death. Principally because it wasn't true. Valerie wasn't pregnant when she died, neither – so far as my mother was ever able to discover – was there an abortion. After my mother caught them having sex, my parents went to see Susan Ward, Valerie's mother – she was a single mother … father, apparently, unknown – and she was adamant that her daughter wasn't pregnant. She even went so far as to accuse my brother of fantasizing. There was no mention of a pregnancy at the inquest into Valerie's death, either. My mother concluded that the girl was a tease and that in effect, it was a wicked lie that she had told my brother for reasons best known to herself.'

Mrs Charles was silent for a moment. 'Was there ever any question of Valerie seeking something – money, perhaps, as a form of blackmail – from your brother because of this alleged pregnancy?'

'If there was, my mother never mentioned it to me. I somehow don't think so. From what my mother had to say of the girl, I think she really was a tease – she would have said something like that to Bernard, who was inclined to take life very seriously and was very much a worrier, just for the fun of it … to see what sort of reaction she'd get from him. He refused to believe my parents when they told him it was all a lie: he wanted to believe Valerie was pregnant and that he was the father of the child. As I've said, at no time was there ever any mention of an abortion, at the inquest or otherwise, but he nevertheless convinced himself that our parents had paid for one to be carried out. They rowed bitterly over it.'

'He obviously loved the girl very much,' Mrs Charles observed.

'I don't really know. My mother said that if it hadn't been for the fact that Valerie knew it herself, she would have been an incredibly beautiful girl. Whatever that means!'

'Does your mother have any idea why Jo Sowerby was so obsessed by her death?'

'No, not really. Mrs Sowerby and Susan Ward were very close, though. That might have had something to do with it. I understand from my mother, that they – Mrs Sowerby and Susan Ward – grew up together in the same children's home and that Susan Ward, in particular, had a tough time of it there. My mother and Susan Ward were in the same class at school; not close friends, but they knew one another fairly well. Mrs Sowerby was a good few years older, I believe, and sort of mothered Susan Ward who died not long after Valerie. My mother said she was fragile, physically and emotionally, even as a child, and was always off from school sick with one thing or another, and that Valerie's death was the finish of her. She never got over it; caught pneumonia after suffering a cold and never recovered. It could explain why Jo Sowerby felt she had to – well, I don't know – make more of Valerie's death than it was. Maybe she felt guilty in some way because she hadn't taken better care of her friend. Who knows?'

There was a small silence, and then Amelia said, 'I was about to say that Valerie's accident ruined so many lives, but I'm not sure that this is strictly true. It was Jo Sowerby who did that, ruined people's lives, when she couldn't let go. The Tomlinson family had to move to New Zealand to get away from her – Andrew Tomlinson was one of the boys there at the gravel pit with Valerie that day. Jonathon Lewis was another one. My mother said he and his family moved from Gidding for the same reason ... to Africa, I believe, as aid workers of one kind or another – to get away from Jo Sowerby, and my brother died, in his case, admittedly, probably from thinking he had a broken heart. The only two who remained in Gidding, are Jo Sowerby's son, Barry, and Cheryl Baxter, the girl who was suspected of having deliberately pushed Valerie down into the gravel pit to her death. My mother said the Baxters stayed put as a matter of principle ... that if they'd moved to get away from the gossip and speculation, it would have looked as if Cheryl was guilty. And now, when there should be an end once and for all to what happened, it has started again. With you and all these questions.'

'I am truly sorry about that,' said Mrs Charles.

'But not sorry enough,' Amelia remarked in a bitter voice, rising to her feet to leave. 'I can't ask you to do what Jo Sowerby should have done years ago and let go, can I?'

'No,' Mrs Charles admitted. 'For me, letting go isn't an option. Not until I uncover the truth.'

Amelia had started to walk away. Mrs Charles called her back. 'There is just one more question I would like to ask, if you wouldn't mind, Mrs Blankhert.'

Amelia turned and looked at her; waited.

'Did your mother ever express an opinion to you about Cheryl Baxter, whether or not she thought Cheryl might have pushed Valerie into the gravel pit?'

Amelia paused for a moment before replying. 'My mother always referred to Cheryl as "that little madam".' And then, turning away, she added: 'Whatever that means.'

Chapter Twenty

'MERTON WAS HOPPING MAD WHEN IT FILTERED BACK TO HIM THAT you'd been in touch with Mrs Watson: I'd keep a very low profile around him for some time to come, if I were you,' David Sayer advised Edwina Charles the following day.

'Her daughter,' Mrs Charles corrected him. 'I met and talked to her daughter. I didn't speak to Mrs Watson direct.'

'The same difference,' he said with a scowl. 'You've gone too far on this one, Madame.'

The clairvoyant looked at him thoughtfully for a moment or two. 'All but two ran away,' she said. 'That's certainly how it looks to me, anyway. Did you know that?'

'What are you talking about?'

'The young people at the gravel pit on the day of the accident. They and their families packed their bags and moved away. The only two who remained to face the music, as it were, were the accused, Cheryl Baxter, and Jo Sowerby's son. One family took on aid work in Africa, another emigrated, as you already know, to New Zealand, and Bernard Watson committed suicide.'

David was shaking his head. 'You're determined to make something of this, aren't you?'

Mrs Charles continued as if he hadn't spoken.

'Cheryl Baxter wasn't going anywhere, that would have made her look guilty, and Jo Sowerby definitely wasn't running away and taking her family with her. She was a woman with a new-found mission to avenge what she believed to be the murder of her close friend's daughter. It is this mass exodus of witnesses that I find suspect. I can't help asking myself if the parents of the other boys either knew their sons were withholding some vital evidence about Valerie's death, or they feared there might be something they weren't letting on.'

'In that case, Mrs Watson knew something, or feared something concerning her son's presence that day at the gravel pit,' David pointed out with a faint sneer.

'Mrs Watson did know something no one else did. Her son firmly believed that Valerie was carrying his child.'

'She wasn't pregnant, I know that much,' said David flatly.

'No. And maybe Valerie set him straight that day at the gravel pit and mocked him for having believed her when she'd told him she was pregnant.'

'And?' said David when she fell silent.

'And it was he and not Cheryl Baxter who followed her there and pushed her to her death.'

Cheryl scowled at her fiancé. 'You're sure you've tried everybody?'

'Everybody,' he said with a nod. 'Not one of her friends has seen her for days.'

'Then one of them is lying,' said Cheryl. 'Where else would that silly girl go?'

'They are not lying, Cheryl,' said Barry with a sigh. 'Why should they? They are as puzzled by Linda's disappearance as we are. A couple of them put it very succinctly, I thought, when they said it was the last thing they'd have thought Linda would do, make a spur of the moment decision to take off on her own someplace. She might think about doing something like this, but when it came down to it, she wouldn't do anything, you know that.'

'What about that boyfriend of hers – Eddie, whatever his name is?'

'I asked and no one knows him. They all said the same thing: he sort of singled Linda out; appeared from out of nowhere at this club they often went to, and drifted into their company. His name, Eddie, is as much as any of them knows about him.'

'He singled out Linda?' Cheryl shook her head. 'Never. I don't believe it!'

'That's what they said.'

'You've got to go to the police.'

'What for?'

'That's where she is, Barry. He's got her. And in case it hasn't occurred to you, the man could be a sex maniac, a serial killer … shall I go on?'

'I'll go to the police,' he said.

Chapter Twenty-one

EDWINA CHARLES HAD SCARCELY PUT DOWN THE PHONE WHEN Merton turned up on her front doorstep, breathing smoke and fire as David had predicted moments earlier after forewarning her of the chief superintendent's pending visit to her home.

Barry Kellar had informed the police of his sister's disappearance and, as the minutes and hours had passed with no trace of her, there was, understandably, increasing concern for her safety. David had confessed to the clairvoyant that Merton knew Linda had consulted her. Mrs Charles had assumed that this information had been passed on to the police by her brother, Barry, but David had apologetically admitted to having been the culprit. He had felt obliged, in the circumstances, to let Merton know that the missing girl had been to see her. Barry Kellar had claimed to have known nothing of the consultation when it was mentioned to him.

Merton was in no mood for pleasantries. 'This is a fine mess you've got us all involved in, Madame,' he growled at her. 'You do realize that so far as we are aware, you were probably the last person to see Linda Kellar.'

Mrs Charles thought about this for a moment and then, with a small nod of her head, said, 'Was I?'

'Unless and until someone comes forward and we are informed to the contrary,' he shot back at her irritably. 'That girl is fragile, Madame. In fact, extremely fragile. And I'm not talking about physically. My fear is that something you've said to her has so frightened and depressed her that she's gone and done something extremely foolish. I have appreciated the help that you have given us in the past, but this time you've gone too far. Your meddling is going to end in grief, if it hasn't already.'

'I agree,' said Mrs Charles calmly, 'but only if Linda continues to keep silent about what she knows.'

Merton glowered at her. 'What are you talking about?'

'Linda knows something that I believe could cast an entirely different light on her mother's death.'

He looked at her antagonistically. 'You're not suggesting that Jo Sowerby was murdered, I hope.'

'I'm not suggesting anything, Mr Merton. The suggestion is nevertheless there, though.... That is, if one accepts that Linda is withholding information' – she paused briefly – 'which would have assisted the police with their enquiries.'

'And to what do we owe thanks for this miraculous insight? That clever little pack of cards of yours?'

Mrs Charles ignored the sarcasm. 'Why should Linda be afraid to talk to the police, Mr Merton? And she is afraid, so afraid of this secret knowledge of hers – which, I believe, in some way concerns her mother – that she tried her best to conceal it from the tarot reading I did for her. But it was there, and it is real. Furthermore, if she has a change of mind and ultimately confides in the wrong person, she will definitely pay the price for her earlier silence with her life.'

'Everything you are saying to me, Madame, simply confirms my belief that the girl left here seriously depressed after your tarot reading and has in all probability taken her own life.'

Mrs Charles was shaking her head slowly. 'That would take courage, Mr Merton, courage Linda doesn't have. She is alive and—'

'And?' he said, narrowing his eyes at her when she paused mid-sentence.

'And I believe is being held somewhere....' Mrs Charles looked away from Merton for a moment. Then looking back at him, she said, 'I was going to say against her will by the person I warned her about, someone who poses a great threat to her, but I cannot be sure—'

'Not sure?' he cut in with a sneer. 'Now there's a turn-up for the books.'

'Someone is out there, Mr Merton. Someone, as I have said, who poses a very great threat to Linda Kellar. Of that I *am* sure.'

There was a small silence. And then, with a faintly malicious gleam in his eyes, Merton said, 'It wouldn't be Roy Adams, by any chance, would it?'

She made no comment, merely raised her eyebrows a little.

'He's dead, Madame. Been blasted to death with his own shotgun. It's early days, the police were only notified of the shooting as I was on my way over here to see you, but on the surface of things, he was shot sometime yesterday.'

She gave him a sharp look.

'And before you go running off getting all manner of wild and wonderful ideas in your head about the motive for his killing … one of his elderly neighbours shot him. They've been at daggers drawn for years. They were found together, Adams blasted in the chest, his neighbour, with whom, it would seem, Adams had been arguing fiercely prior to the shooting, lying dead nearby. Adams's neighbour was in his late seventies and had got himself so worked up he'd suffered a fatal stroke.'

'This was after shooting Roy Adams?' she asked, eyeing him thoughtfully.

'There are no sinister plots here, Madame,' sighed Merton. 'This was a straightforward neighbours-from-hell slaying. The old man called round to see Adams for what would appear to have been a fairly regular shouting match about Adams's liking for shooting wildlife, they lost their tempers with one another – as was, apparently, their custom – and then, in a blind rage, the old man snatched up Adams's shotgun and simply let him have it with both barrels.'

'You're sure about that, are you? That Adams's neighbour didn't suffer a stroke as a result of his finding Adams shot to death?'

Merton threw up his hands. 'I give up,' he said. He turned to leave, paused, and then, looking back at the clairvoyant, he said, 'I give you my personal assurance, Madame, that as soon as all the forensic work has been carried out and documented, confirming what I have just told you, you will be among the first to hear the results. And now, if you don't mind, I've got a missing girl to find.'

Chapter Twenty-two

STAN NORTH WASN'T ONE FOR EAVESDROPPING ON OTHER PEOPLE'S conversations unless they were speculating on the weather prospects for the forthcoming week, or commenting on observations made on some aspect of the local environment affecting wildlife in all of its forms.

He had called in at the Post Office Stores first thing the following morning to buy a postage stamp for the letter he had written to the district council, lodging a formal complaint with them and insisting that legal action be taken against one of the local farmers who had cut back the hedgerow bordering the farmer's land much earlier than permitted by law and while wild birds were still nesting. In some distress, Stan had carried home the evidence of the alleged crime – a fledgling, ring-necked dove – which had been savagely butchered by the hedge-cutting machinery and which, he informed the council, he intended to hold for them to inspect at their convenience.

The postmistress was discussing the shooting of Roy Adams with the elderly woman she was serving ahead of Stan. The local morning paper, Gidding's *The Sketch*, had covered the incident in graphic detail. 'He called in here the other day asking about property for sale hereabouts,' she said. 'At least, the photograph in this morning's paper looks very much like him to me ... I'm not likely to forget that shaved head of his, am I? He seemed to think Edwina Charles's bungalow might be up for sale. I can't say I liked the look of him; it all seemed a bit suspicious, as if what he really wanted to know had nothing at all to do with wanting to buy a property and more to do with Mrs Charles....'

Stan thought long and hard about this conversation. That bit about the shaved head rang a discordant bell with him. He didn't normally take *The Sketch*, but he bought a copy on his way out. Privately, he agreed with the postmistress that it was the man – not necessarily who had enquired about property at the Post Office Stores the other day, Stan had not known anything about that – who had definitely been the driver of the car that had all but knocked him down.

This was not all that Stan thought about long and hard. On an inside page there was a photograph of a missing girl, the one Stan clearly remembered escorting across the road and up to Edwina Charles's front door, and the same girl he later saw speaking to the man with the shaved head who had come so close to running over him.

Stan wasn't sure what he should do with this information. He thought about phoning the police; still hadn't made up his mind by lunchtime. He wished the girl hadn't put him in mind of his own daughter, who would be about her age now, and whom he hadn't seen or heard from since his wife left him for another man and took their baby girl, an only child, with her. He decided to give it some more thought while working in the wood at the bottom of Mrs Charles's garden and, as luck would have it – or possibly, as he had hoped – Mrs Charles came out and spoke to him.

'That man who got shot the other side of Gidding,' he said, after they had exchanged greetings and made a general observation on the weather, which was showing signs of turning thundery and wet before nightfall, 'he gave that girl who called on you the other day a lift somewhere ... this was after she'd said goodbye to you and left.'

Mrs Charles gave him a thoughtful look. 'You mean Roy Adams?'

'Yes, I think I remember reading that name in this morning's paper. Had a bald head ... shaved – I don't think he was naturally bald. Nearly ran me down. Can't say I liked the look of him,' he added, echoing the sentiments of the postmistress.

'Are you sure about this, Mr North?'

He looked doubtful. 'Fairly sure. The girl was walking along the road, back towards the village after she left you, and he pulled up … this was after he'd nearly run me over. It looked like … well, I'm not positive about this, but it seemed to me that he might have been trying to make her get into his car. I don't mean physically forcing her into it: I never saw him get out and speak to her, nor lay a finger on her.'

'You actually saw her getting into his car?'

'Well, no. But I'm pretty sure she did. I looked away for a split second and when I looked back, the car and the girl had disappeared. If she'd refused to accept a lift, I would have seen her: she would've still been walking along the road.' He suddenly looked doubtful. 'Wouldn't she?' He hesitated. Then, 'It worried me: I couldn't help thinking it might've been my daughter who was being approached like that.'

He spoke thoughtfully; had turned and was walking away before he had finished speaking.

Mrs Charles watched him with a deeply concerned look in her eye. The farther he got from her, the darker grew the shadow that she could see forming around him in silhouette. If he went to the police with this information about Linda Kellar, and she was inclined to think he would after giving the matter a little more thought, and particularly in relation to his own daughter, he would be faced with serious consequences.

She wanted to call him back and warn him to think carefully about any decision he might make in regard to contacting the police about what he had seen, but she knew she couldn't; she mustn't interfere. The girl had to be found, and if Stan North's information would help the police in their search for her, then Stan had to tell them what he had seen.

Chapter Twenty-three

CHERYL WATCHED BARRY WORKING ON THE CROSSWORD PUZZLE IN *The Sketch. How could he sit there so calmly?* she asked herself angrily when, for her part, she was almost at screaming point.

Barry was actually anything but calm. He normally completed this particular crossword in five minutes flat. Tonight he simply couldn't concentrate on it. The lines of questions kept either running away from him off the page, or the harder he stared at them, the more blurred and incomprehensible they became.

He was sick with worry, not that he would have admitted this to Cheryl. He had done the right thing and had gone to the police, checked out all of Linda's friends. What more could he do? The police had hinted that maybe Linda had been so depressed at having found her mother dead that she had taken her life. He couldn't say that he had noticed any obvious signs of depression in his sister, but then she wasn't living there at the flat with him and Cheryl, was she? She'd preferred to stay on in the family home until it was sold; said she wasn't bothered about being there on her own.

The inference that she was depressed by their mother's death had taken him by surprise. He wouldn't have said that Linda and their mother were close, but then Linda was a strange girl; kept all her thoughts and feelings to herself, always had. Maybe she'd been more deeply affected than he had suspected.

And then there was that visit to a clairvoyant.... The police seemed to find that very significant so far as the present state of Linda's mental health was concerned.

Cheryl suddenly spoke. 'I don't know how you can sit there so calmly when you know your sister's gone missing. First your mother dies, then Linda disappears, and now Roy Adams has gone and got himself shot. It doesn't seem to have occurred to you that our lives are slowly unravelling before our eyes. We're supposed to be getting married in less than a month's time, and it's just one thing after another. What next, I wonder?'

He looked up at her. 'Getting upset isn't going to help anybody, is it, Cheryl?' he said. He looked down at the crossword again. 'I'm sure the last thing my mother would've wanted was to spoil everything for us by having a heart attack and dying so close to our wedding day. It wasn't deliberate.'

'That wasn't; it's Linda I'm not so sure about.'

He looked up at her and something, only very briefly, like real dislike showed in his eyes. Cheryl saw it and said, defensively, 'Well, how can you be sure that she hasn't deliberately gone missing in the hope that we'll postpone the wedding?'

'Linda would know I'd be worried and upset about her, that's how I know she hasn't deliberately gone missing to spite you. Be sensible, Cheryl: why should she want us to postpone our wedding?'

'It doesn't seem to me that she's particularly excited about it.'

'Only because lately you hardly talk of much else.' He sighed. 'Look, stop worrying, will you? The police will find her. She won't have gone far. She'd need some real money for that and she hasn't any. Not so far as I'm aware.' He went on with the crossword.

It was a muggy evening after a brief burst of thundery rain late in the afternoon and Cheryl's skin felt hot and clammy. Barry had opened the window to let in some fresh air and the beaded cord on the blind was striking the reveal in a slight breeze. The repetitive sound it was making was getting on her nerves.

'What if it's got something to do with Roy Adams?' she said with a worried frown. 'I'm absolutely positive that she was seeing him behind your back.'

He raised his eyebrows at her. 'What do you mean? Linda went missing before he got shot and anyway, that wouldn't have upset her enough to make her run away.'

'Maybe she was feeling guilty for not telling you he'd been coming to the house.'

'Knowing him, the chances are she didn't have much say in the matter.' *Dear me*, he thought, *this isn't how it's going to be for the rest of our lives, is it? Cheryl expecting me to keep tabs on Linda's every thought and action?*

'And you're going to have to do something about this clairvoyant business,' she went on sharply. 'We need to know what that was all about.'

He looked up at her again. There were times, and this was one of them, when he had a feeling that Cheryl was holding out on him about something and that in this instance, it wasn't so much Linda she was concerned about as Cheryl herself. 'Whatever for?'

'It was out of character: Linda would never think of doing something like that.'

Privately, he agreed with her, it *was* a strange thing for Linda to do, but he wasn't going to admit it to her.

'What if something she's been told by this clairvoyant has upset and frightened her?' Cheryl continued, after a small pause.

'She'll turn up soon and you can ask her yourself. Maybe going to see a clairvoyant had something to do with a project she's working on – for when she goes to college.'

Cheryl had to resist an urge to shout at Barry that if this were an example of the way he was thinking, then he badly needed a wake-up call. It so happened she had just the thing, something she hadn't been going to tell him, but now she would. 'You might be interested to know that a reporter from *The Sketch* called at the agency to see me this morning,' she said.

He looked up at her. 'What did he want?'

'He started by asking about Linda, how you and I felt about her having gone missing – he said he'd been assigned the job of looking into her disappearance – and then all of a sudden, he wanted to know what I thought about Roy Adams. I mean, about what happened to him.'

Barry widened his eyes at her; said nothing. He could see she hadn't finished.

'He wasn't very old – probably only in his early twenties – but he seemed to know everything there was to know about your mother and Roy, going back years.'

'If you think about it, I guess it was only to be expected. I wouldn't worry about it.'

'That's easier said than done, Barry. You don't seem to understand where all this is leading—' She broke off; she was saying too much, more than she had intended.

He looked at her for a very long moment without saying anything. 'Is there something you're not telling me?'

'No, of course not. But can't you see, now that Linda's gone missing, so soon after your mother's death and Roy Adams managing to get himself killed, there'll be reporters everywhere – when we get married, I mean; and it won't be us they're interested in, will it? It will be Cheryl Baxter and Valerie Ward. Everything's always been about Valerie, ever since she died,' she finished bitterly.

'Stop it, Cheryl!' he said sternly.

'It's all right for you to say that. What if he keeps probing? He's the sort who will.'

'You're talking about this young reporter, right?'

She nodded.

'If there'd been anything there to find out, my mother and Roy Adams would have found it years ago. There's nothing there, Cheryl. Don't *you* start!'

'What if…?' Cheryl hesitated. She could feel anger rising in her chest, which was becoming painfully tight, and something else as well: real fear. What she had just said was true: their lives were unravelling and Barry couldn't, or wouldn't, see it. 'What if I told you I pushed her, Barry?' Now that she had started, the words came tumbling out; she couldn't hold them back. 'Your mother knows I pushed her, and don't you dare pretend that you never knew this. I could see it in your mother's eyes every time she looked at me. She hated me, you know she hated me. It was all pretence with her. She just hoped that by standing back and having nothing to say to me directly, I'd finally cave in and tell her what she wanted to hear.'

There was a long silence. It was true what she'd said about his mother, but that had been something they had been going to have to live with. It was the rest of what she'd said that didn't make any sense to Barry. *What?* After all these years, all the denial, Cheryl was admitting that she deliberately pushed Valerie into the gravel pit?

'What are you trying to say, Cheryl?' The odd look in her eyes, almost a look of quiet triumph, was making him feel increasingly uneasy. It even flashed into his mind that all that had happened over the past week or so, on top of the pressures of the wedding, had pushed her over the edge into some sort of nervous breakdown. She had seemed much more in control since his mother had died, almost a different person, but now he wondered if it hadn't been an act and underneath it all, she was the same watchfully wary Cheryl she'd turned into since that day at the gravel pit.

'I went back, Barry.' Cheryl turned her head a little on one side and looked at him thoughtfully. She had to do something to make him sit up and take notice of her, and she felt much calmer now that she had finally got his complete attention. 'I've never told anybody this, not even my parents, and nobody ever thought to ask me that one simple question: if I went back to the gravel pit a second time to see if Valerie was all right after I'd pushed her, so I kept quiet about it. I knew what people would think if I'd admitted I'd gone back. They've thought it, anyway. Everybody thinks I killed Valerie.' The strange little smile on Cheryl's lips was chilling. 'She was alive, Barry: I saw her crawling up the side of the pit on all fours like a scared little puppy-dog and panting like mad. So undignified, it was all I could do not to laugh. She was almost up to the top when I turned away, and she shouted at me … called me a spiteful little bitch and that she'd make me pay for what I'd done to her. It must have been after I'd walked away that second time that she lost her footing and slipped down the side again and this time right into the water.'

She looked at him for a moment. 'Do you know what, Barry? I've half a mind to put an end to all of this and tell the police I went back. I'm sick to death of it. I only wish I'd told the police this before your mother and Roy Adams died. Maybe then they'd have left me in peace.'

'How do you make that out? They still wouldn't have believed you. They wanted you to be guilty. You would've simply played into their hands. If you want my advice, you should do what you've always done and what you should've done now; kept your mouth shut. You say Valerie was OK the last time you saw her; I believe you. I don't want to hear any more about it. It's done, finished! Drop it. Right now! You're going to make yourself ill, carrying on like this.'

'I think one of us should—'

He shook out the paper irritably; looked down at the cross-word again. 'Not another word, Cheryl. As far as I'm concerned this conversation never took place.'

But it did take place, Barry; and if you're content to sit there night after night with a stupid crossword puzzle and refuse to do something, thought Cheryl, *I will. Valerie Ward, your mother, Roy Adams and now your sister never succeeded in standing in my way in the past, and trust me, no one is going to in the future. Particularly that clairvoyant after what that reporter told me about her today....*

Chapter Twenty-four

LINDA WAS SHIVERY, FELT AS IF SHE HAD A COLD COMING ON, BUT thought it was more likely to be nerves. She was on her own. Eddie had gone off to work half an hour ago, saying he expected to be back at around 1.30 a.m. and that she was not to wait up for him. She was trying to make up her mind whether she shouldn't go home and see if there weren't some means of contacting Barry without Cheryl's knowing. It would be Cheryl to whom she would have to account for herself: Barry would be far less demanding, permitting her to take things at her own pace and talk to him about where she had been when she was ready.

The previous night she had slept downstairs on a foldaway bed tucked down one side of Eddie's grandmother's small dining-table. He had accompanied her upstairs each time she had needed to use the bathroom, reminding her uncomfortably of Roy Adams, although Eddie hadn't been waiting outside the door with cleaning equipment to mop up after her as Roy had. Eddie had apologized to her for this, insisting that it was necessary if he were to make sure that his grandmother didn't know she was there. Linda had accepted this explanation without question, was just grateful not to have been turned away, and had promised him that she wouldn't do anything – make any noise or go upstairs while he was out, she had meant – that would cause his grandmother any distress.

She hadn't seen much of Eddie during the day, he had kept disappearing for prolonged periods of time without once bothering to tell her where he was going. The third time it had happened, she had begun to ask herself if he were avoiding her, or was maybe trying to tell her something. While both scenarios had seemed embarrassingly distinct possibilities, she would nevertheless have delayed any decision about returning home until the following day at least. This was if it hadn't been for the newspaper that Eddie had left lying about casually where he knew she was sure to see it.

He had known all along that she had been talking about Roy Adams. The newspaper had been left folded in such a way that Roy's face and the report of his death, together with a passing reference to his connection with her mother and the accidental death of Valerie Ward eleven years ago, were staring straight up at her. She knew what it meant. Eddie was pointing out to her that there was now no reason for her not to return home. She didn't handle the newspaper; simply read it where it lay. Had she opened it, she would have discovered a photograph of herself with a report that she had gone missing.

Linda had slept so heavily the previous night, she had been completely unaware of any activity upstairs. Both nights, Eddie had taken a tray up to his grandmother at around seven o'clock, had brought it down an hour later with a knife and fork placed neatly across an empty plate and a dessertspoon left all alone in the pudding bowl he'd taken up. The cup of tea that had also gone up on the tray, had returned, drained empty of all but a few scattered tea leaves that were sticking to the sides and on the bottom of it. The same ritual had taken place that morning at breakfast, but again with little or no sound coming from upstairs other than for the soft murmurings of Eddie's voice. Linda hadn't been able to pick out any other voice in the conversation that he had been having, and after a long day of thinking things over, she had finally reached the conclusion that it was all a sham. Nobody was up there: Eddie had been talking to himself, knowing that she would be able to hear his voice and believe him when he said there was someone other than the two of them in the house. This was why he didn't want her wandering about up there on her own.

She didn't know what to make of any of it. Why lie to her about having a grandmother he cared for? – and he had lied about that, right from the night they had first met. She had also thought that now and again she had caught him looking at her strangely, as if trying to make up his mind about something. She couldn't understand that, either.

She decided to leave. He was right: there was no reason now why she shouldn't. The police knew who had shot Roy – that neighbour he'd mentioned to her, the one he was always quarrelling with. She had nothing to fear from the police. No one was ever going to know that she'd been anywhere near Roy's place the day he had died, let alone heard the shot that had killed him. Out in the hall, though, she paused. She looked thoughtfully at the staircase. *Why not?* she asked herself, creeping up them slowly. If, for some reason, Eddie suddenly turned up, she'd say she had needed to use the bathroom urgently; couldn't wait for him to come home.

The first door she tried at the top of the stairs opened on to what was probably Eddie's room, the second door, which wasn't quite closed and she nudged open cautiously with the toe of her shoe, brought a small gasp of shock to her lips. For one dreadful moment, she thought her knees were going to buckle beneath her and dump her in a heap on the floor.

The old lady sitting in a comfortable armchair, peering through a thick magnifying glass on a stand at some needlework that was stretched taut on a round wooden frame, looked up at her suddenly.

'Oh, it's you, Marama,' said the old lady. 'Be a dear and pick up my glasses for me, will you? I've knocked them on the floor. I'm always knocking things on the floor. One of the penalties of getting old, I'm afraid.'

Linda crossed to her reluctantly, picking up her spectacles, which were lying at the old lady's feet, and then handing them to her.

'He's gone off to that awful job of his, has he?' asked the old lady, rubbing her eyes with the fingers of both hands, as if suffering from severe eyestrain.

'*Er*, yes,' said Linda. 'About half an hour ago. He said he'd be back soon after one o'clock.'

The old lady blinked furiously for a moment or two and then squinted myopically at her. 'Your voice sounds funny. What's wrong with it?'

'I, *er*, I'm tired, that's all.'

'No stamina, you young people. I could murder another cup of tea. You wouldn't mind rustling one up for me, would you, dear?'

'No, *um*, no, of course not.' Linda backed towards the door. She was beginning to shake. 'I won't be long.'

'You're sure there's nothing wrong with your voice, Marama?'

'No, no, it's fine.'

Linda turned and fled, straight down the stairs and out of the front door.

Marama! Who was Marama?

She was asking herself the same question when she finally got home and began searching through her shoulder bag for her house keys.

An ex-girlfriend?

No, Marama wasn't an ex. The way Eddie's grandmother had spoken her name seemed to pinpoint her as being more of the moment, and that she was still a very definite presence in both Eddie and his grandmother's lives. It somehow made sense to Linda that he had a girlfriend, someone he was prepared to introduce to his grandmother who obviously knew her very well, bearing in mind that remark she'd made about the change in her voice. What Linda didn't understand was why Eddie had picked her out of the crowd that first night they'd met. He had made her feel really special.

Just thinking about it made her cringe inside. It had been so deliberate; hadn't seemed so at the time, but that was what it was. For some reason, he'd picked her out deliberately.

She opened her bag a little wider. She couldn't find her keys, they were gone. That meant....

She thought she was going to be sick.

She had somehow lost them while she was with Roy Adams, after he'd left her in the horse box and had gone off somewhere in his car, hadn't she? There was nothing attached to them to say they were her keys, though, was there? This was if the police searched the horse box for some reason and found them and wanted to know to whom they belonged.

No, *it couldn't have been while she was in the horse box, waiting for Roy to come back.*

She paused for a moment, her face reddening and her heart pounding painfully in her breast. She had gone to her bag for a tissue and had felt the keys while she was rummaging about in there. This was while she was walking back into town. That meant she had either dragged the keys out with the tissue without realizing, and had lost them on the way.

Or....

She looked round fearfully over her shoulder at the steadily darkening night that was creeping stealthily up on her.

Or Eddie had taken them from her bag last night while she was asleep.

That was ridiculous! Why would he?

Chapter Twenty-five

'MY GOD, LINDA, CHERYL AND I HAVE BEEN GOING OUT OF OUR minds with worry! Where on earth have you been?'

Linda looked at her brother with a small frown. 'Walking.'

'What do you mean, *walking*?' Barry asked her irritably, stepping back from the door of the flat for her to come in.

She didn't move. She was looking past him, into the dimly lit hallway beyond. He guessed what was bothering her.

'She's not here, Linda. Her mother phoned a short while ago: she's not feeling very well and Cheryl's gone round to see her.' He studied his sister's face. *There was someone else who didn't look as if she was feeling very well!* Linda was white as a sheet and the dark shadows under her eyes were damp with perspiration. 'This whole business,' he went on, 'Mum and now Roy Adams, has really got to all of us, you know. Roy Adams's shooting has shaken Mrs Baxter up badly: it's brought back a whole load of bad memories. You know about that, of course ... that Roy Adams has been shot? By one of his neighbours, it said in the paper.'

She didn't answer him. 'I'm sorry, Barry; I've lost my keys. Can you lend me yours until I get some new ones cut?'

'Don't you want to come in?'

Linda shook her head. 'I'm very tired. I just want to go home and go to bed.'

'Are you going to tell me where you've been?'

She shook her head again.

'You're not in some sort of trouble, are you?' he asked her with a thoughtful frown.

'No, of course not. I'm fine. I just wanted a bit of time on my own for a while ... to think.'

'I'll get my keys. But we've got to talk, Linda. Tomorrow ... OK? This can't go on. Cheryl is getting very upset, what with the wedding and everything, and I don't mind telling you, we were absolutely stunned when the police told me you'd been to see a clairvoyant. What the devil was that all about?'

'Mum. It was her idea, not mine. She thought that if I saw a clairvoyant, it would help me to make up my mind about what I should do next, whether I should go on to college or not.'

He looked mildly surprised. 'That doesn't sound like Mum. She liked to be in complete control.' His eyebrows went up. 'Well, did it work?'

'No, of course it didn't. It was a crazy idea.'

Barry couldn't have agreed more.

Linda looked at her brother hesitantly. 'You've been to the police? About me?'

'Of course I've been to the police. What did you expect when you suddenly disappeared the way you did, without a word to anybody? Anything could've happened to you. A reporter from *The Sketch* somehow got hold of the story, too. The police, I expect. I'll have to do something quickly and let everybody know that you've turned up safe and sound. But don't be surprised if the police want to know where you've been. They've been searching everywhere for you; we all have.'

'I'm sorry. I didn't mean to cause all this trouble.'

'I'll get my keys and see you home.' *Knowing you, Linda, left to your own devices, you're just as likely to go missing again!*

He kept the thought to himself. He had enough problems. Linda's mind had always worked in mysterious ways, and if Cheryl was right and she had been seeing Roy Adams behind their backs, she might well have been off on some kind of guilt trip for having kept it to herself. His death so soon after their mother's – assuming she'd got to know of it – had probably thrown her a bit off-balance: it was perfectly reasonable to think that she might've needed some time and space on her own while she got her head around it.

Giving his head a slow shake, Barry turned to go and get the house keys.

Chapter Twenty-six

'I AM BEGINNING TO THINK THAT I'VE MADE A GRAVE MISTAKE IN agreeing to Jo Sowerby's request for a tarot reading,' Edwina Charles confessed to her brother early the following morning.

Cyril looked vague, after a moment or two, nodded his head. His sister doubted that he would remember that the late Jo Sowerby had been to see her. His memory span was notoriously short, anything going back beyond several minutes could generally be counted on to be gone forever. She went on, accepting that she was speaking her thoughts out loud and to herself: 'I was thinking of calling on Coopers, the florists, in town today to see if they could throw some light on the person who sent the floral tributes you remembered seeing that day at the Baxters' birthday party.'

He nodded his head again, but she was quite sure that he hadn't heard a word she'd said. 'But then I remembered,' she continued, 'the Coopers sold the business some years ago, didn't they? To a local garden centre that wanted a shop in town. I think it very unlikely that the new owners would have a record of the transaction after all this time, and I doubt that it would be worth my while trying either of the other two Gidding florists. They aren't as central as the old Coopers shop was, are they?'

'Yes,' he said. He got up from the sofa where he had been sitting, gripping his knees and with his brooding gaze fixed on some spot on his sister's open sitting-room doorway, as if calculating the length of time involved and the distance he would need to cross before he would reach it and be free to leave.

He stood perfectly still for a moment – for all the world, his sister thought, as if trying to remember what he had intended to do next. 'I know Joyce Cooper's address, if that's any use to you,' he said.

She looked at him thoughtfully. 'It was her business, was it?'

Cyril narrowed his eyes at his sister. 'I just said so, didn't I? Haven't you been listening to me?'

'I'm sorry, Cyril,' she apologized, seizing the moment and quickly fetching a notepad and pen from the writing bureau. 'I've had such a lot on my mind lately, I'm finding it extremely difficult to concentrate on anything.' She held the pen poised, ready to note down the address she hoped her brother remembered offering to give her.

It was an address in Gidding and he dictated it slowly and carefully to her, as if expecting her to look up at him at any moment and ask him why she needed it.

'Thank you, Cyril: you've been most helpful.'

He nodded his agreement and crossed to the door. There he paused, and then, looking back at his sister, he said, 'You won't find her there, though. Not today. She'll be at the cathedral for most of the day, arranging flowers.'

'It's Wednesday, Cyril.'

He gave her a strange look. 'Yes.'

'Joyce Cooper arranges the flowers in Gidding Cathedral on Wednesdays? Are you sure about this, Cyril?'

'They squabble about it, who's going to arrange the flowers – the women on the flower roster,' he explained when his sister looked at him thoughtfully. 'They've been squabbling about it for as long as I can remember. They don't like it when Joyce does them: they've tried for years to get her to quit. She knows it and won't budge ... laughs about it behind their backs. They're jealous of her because she's a professional florist and they aren't.'

As a fairly regular attendant at Sunday mass at the cathedral, and a former choirmaster there, Mrs Charles was inclined to think that her brother knew what he was talking about, and that she could therefore reasonably expect to find the florist she needed to speak to about the funeral that never was, busy in the cathedral that day if she decided to make a trip into town to see her. She smiled to herself. One last check, though, just to be on the safe side.

She didn't get the chance.

'I thought you said you'd made a mistake in getting involved with that woman who wanted you to read the tarot for her.' Cyril spoke challengingly, fixing his sister with one of his dark, brooding looks. 'I'd leave well enough alone, if I were you.'

'I'm trying to save someone's life, Cyril. The problem is, I don't know whose.'

The vaguely puzzled look that came slowly into his eyes warned Mrs Charles that his thinking processes had wandered off at a tangent, and not entirely unpredictably. 'Someone's out to get Joyce Cooper because she won't take the hint and give up arranging the flowers – is that what's been worrying you?'

Mrs Charles sighed to herself. She was about to assure Cyril that so far as she was concerned, there was absolutely no threat whatsoever to the florist's life in relation to what she increasingly suspected was the murder of Jo Sowerby.

But she couldn't be sure about that, could she?

Chapter Twenty-seven

A SMALL STAB OF IRRITATION WENT THROUGH DAVID SAYER WHEN HE caught a quick glimpse of Edwina Charles standing outside her front gate. He had hoped to drive past her bungalow this morning with no more than a quick wave of greeting – this was in the event that he had caught sight of her – and it be left at that for today; was further irritated when, as his car drew nearer, she took a step forward, as if expecting him to slow to a stop and speak to her. He had confessed to his wife, Jean, that his role of go-between and peacemaker was beginning to wear a bit thin, and that he had to agree with Clive Merton that Edwina Charles was fast becoming a meddlesome busybody who would do better to confine her dubious talents to those who had the time and money to indulge themselves in her particular brand of nonsense. As Clive Merton had said to him the last time they had spoken, she couldn't be right all the time, no one was, and she definitely wasn't right this time about Jo Sowerby.

'Good morning,' she called to him cheerfully, as he leaned across to speak to her through the open, front passenger-side window. 'I wonder if I might beg a ride into Gidding with you, Superintendent?'

'No new dramatic developments in the Sowerby saga, then?' he enquired. He couldn't resist it once their conversation, which had centred on the weather prospects for the day, had petered out.

Mrs Charles was silent for a moment or two. Then she said, 'No, I don't think so.'

Thank God for that! he thought.

They spent the rest of the drive into Gidding discussing his aunt, who had phoned him at eight o'clock that morning, complaining of feeling unwell.

'It's actually more to do with fear than anything,' he said. 'She's getting on in years and living alone is beginning to frighten her when she has these little episodes of not feeling her sparkling best. Jean and I want her to move into Gidding to be nearer to us when these little emergencies of hers arise, but she won't hear of it. She was born here in the village, in the cottage she's lived in all her life, and that's where she plans on dying. Never mind what all this toing and froing is doing to me. She's wearing me out!' He smiled wryly. 'And I apologize if I've seemed a bit short-tempered this morning, but where my aunt is concerned, it goes with the territory.'

Mrs Charles glanced at him. 'Dare I risk asking if there has been any news of Linda Kellar?'

'I haven't spoken to Merton for a day or two, so I don't really know what's going on there. I didn't get much of a chance to look at the paper before I drove over to see my aunt this morning, but I would imagine that there's still been no word of her. I personally would say things are definitely beginning to look rather black for that young lady. Mispers – missing persons, that is – usually turn up quicker than this, that's if they are going to.'

They were approaching the centre of town where Mrs Charles had asked to be dropped off.

'Perhaps,' she said after a small silence, 'the next time you see Mr Merton, you might like to mention to him that it might be worthwhile getting someone to have a word with Stan North.'

She frowned to herself. She had got it wrong about Stan. He clearly hadn't contacted the police about what he had seen the day Linda had called on her, as she had expected: David would have made some mention of it. That made her an accessory to the withholding of vital information, this was if what Stan had witnessed taking place between Linda and Roy Adams proved to have some definite relevance to the girl's disappearance. Mrs Charles wished there were some alternative, but there wasn't: she simply had to risk that she was also wrong about the effect Stan's inevitable involvement now with the police would have on his life.

David shot her a quick look. 'A brief history of the life and times of the dung beetle, or whatever, would be about the last thing Merton would be interested in right now.'

Mrs Charles gave a thoughtful nod. 'I dare say. He may, however, like to know that I might not have been the last person to see Linda, as he has suggested to me. There's a slight possibility that Stan North was ... while he was busy in the hedgerows that day. Mr North seemed to me to be reasonably sure that he saw Linda – this was after she'd left me – speaking to Roy Adams and then getting into his car and driving off with him.'

Chapter Twenty-eight

JOYCE COOPER WAS ARRANGING FLOWERS ON THE ALTAR IN GIDDING Cathedral's Lady Chapel. Edwina Charles took a seat on a pew and waited until she had finished, standing up as Joyce gathered up the slightly withered and drooping flowers from the floral arrangement she was replacing, and then turned to leave. She paused on seeing the clairvoyant and gave her a friendly smile. She was a small woman, probably in her early seventies, with noticeably thick ankles and a certain awkwardness of movement which suggested that there was a problem with her hips.

'It is Mrs Cooper, isn't it?' said Mrs Charles with a smile. 'I've been admiring your handiwork. The flowers are lovely.'

'I'm afraid it's been a difficult summer for flowers. Too much rain. But I do the best with what I've got.' She looked at Mrs Charles thoughtfully. 'I'm sorry, should I know you? I mean, you know who I am, and I confess that my memory these days, particularly for faces and names, is appalling. The perils of growing old,' she added with a cheerful grin.

'No, we haven't met, but I believe you know my brother, Cyril Forbes. He told me I might find you here today.'

Joyce Cooper nodded. 'Ah, yes: 'Del, isn't it? Your brother has mentioned you on one or two occasions and I know of you, of course, quite independently of Cyril, through your reputation as a highly regarded clairvoyant.'

Joyce placed the flowers she was carrying, on a pew and then shook hands with Mrs Charles. 'I'm very pleased to meet you at long last. Your brother has a remarkable voice. We were all very sorry when he decided to quit the choir.' She smiled. 'I don't suppose there's any chance that you could persuade him to have a rethink?'

'Unfortunately, no,' replied Mrs Charles. 'His voice, in his opinion, isn't what it was, and as he doesn't feel he can any longer give of his best, he prefers to stay in retirement and pursue his other interests.' She went on, 'I was hoping you might be able to assist me with some background information I need if I am to help a young girl who has come to me with a serious problem of a terrifying recurring nightmare which, I have reason to believe, has its origins in something that happened some seven or so years ago at a children's party held by the Baxter family here in Gidding.'

'Don't remind me,' said Joyce wryly. 'It gave me a nightmare or two, I don't mind telling you…. But before you go any further, I'll have to take the weight off these tin hips of mine and sit down. Like me, they're cracking on a bit now and beginning to feel their age.'

They both sat down. Then Joyce went on, 'I warn you, my memory's not what was, and really, my best recall of the incident that I'm pretty sure you're referring to, can be summed up in two words – total embarrassment. Nothing like that had ever happened before or has ever happened to me again, although a florist friend of mine who has a business in Nottingham experienced something similar as a result of a lovers' tiff. Most unpleasant for all concerned and all very silly, although in my case, what happened to the Baxter family was horribly malicious and, as I've said, for me, extremely embarrassing.'

'Do you know who placed the order with you for the floral tributes that were delivered to the Baxters' home?'

'No.' Joyce shook her head. 'The police couldn't trace who'd ordered them, either. It was a phone and cash transaction. A woman made the phone call early in the morning, ordering an incredible number of wreaths and sheaves and giving me an address for delivery for late that afternoon. I confess that at first, I thought it was some kind of hoax, this was because of the size of the order, but then a man called into the shop about twenty minutes later and paid for the lot in cash.'

'Did you know the man?'

Joyce shook her head. 'I couldn't even describe him to you, not now. I seem to remember thinking, though, that I'd seen him somewhere before.' She shrugged. 'Collecting flowers from the shop ... he was a messenger, some sort of delivery man ... a taxi driver, maybe. I'd given the woman who'd phoned a quote for the flowers, the delivery man had the right money, didn't want a receipt, and was gone in a flash. I think the police checked out the delivery and taxi services in town, but I'm not sure. Anyway, I never heard any more about it, so I would imagine they drew a blank there, too. After all, the delivery man could've come from just about anywhere, even from one of the overnight delivery services from another part of the country.'

'Not if he arrived at your shop to pay for the flowers twenty minutes after you'd received the order.'

Joyce nodded. 'No, of course not. Silly me! The delivery man, whoever he was, had to be in cahoots with the woman who'd placed the order with me.'

Mrs Charles thought for a moment and then rose to her feet. Joyce looked up at her. 'I haven't been of much help, have I?'

'It was all a long time ago, it was asking a lot to expect you to remember back that far, but thank you, anyway, for talking to me. I won't keep you from your work any longer.'

Joyce had remained seated. 'There were a lot of rumours flying around at the time about who was behind the ordering of the flowers and what it was all about, and while I would like to think that as a good Christian woman' – she smiled faintly and cast her eyes heavenwards, as if seeking absolution – 'I did feel that I had something of a vested interest in listening to the whispers.'

Mrs Charles sat down again. She waited.

'Valerie Ward—?' Joyce paused, waiting for some reaction from Mrs Charles and then, when Mrs Charles nodded, continued, 'She used to work for me ... well, I say *worked*, but that would've been breaking the law as she was under-age. She *helped* me in the shop – had a natural talent for flower arranging. The whispers I heard were about that accident she had. Please don't quote me on any of this, but a great many people in town were utterly convinced that Cheryl Baxter, the elder sister of the little girl whose birthday party was spoilt by the delivery of flowers for a funeral, had deliberately pushed Valerie into the water where she drowned. Another rumour was that a close friend of Valerie's mother and the delivery man who called at my shop to pay for the flowers – one of the detectives investigating Valerie's death who, I believe, I can remember someone mentioning to me, resigned over the case – were responsible for ordering them from me. Just rumours, of course.... For my part, though, I wasn't entirely convinced by what people were saying about the identity of the delivery man: I would've said he was a younger man, but I'm not sure, it might've been the detective ... I honestly don't know,' she finished with a lop-sided smile.

'Cyril was hired to entertain the children at the Baxters' party with a performance of Punch and Judy and some magic, so I have some idea of when all of this happened, but I wonder if you can remember how long it was after Valerie Ward had died that you received that order for the flowers?'

Joyce closed her eyes for a moment. Then she said, 'I'm not really sure.... It's just a guess – three, maybe four years later. Something like that.'

Mrs Charles nodded, as if agreeing that this assumption tallied with her understanding of the time lapse involved. She was silent for a moment. Then she said, 'Valerie Ward – what happened to her at the gravel pit and the general belief that Cheryl Baxter was in some way responsible for it – is at the root of my sitter's problem ... more so, I have reason to think, than the nightmares she is suffering. Had Valerie not died in the way she did, the upset at the birthday party would never have occurred. Would you be prepared to tell me what you, as someone who had close contact with the girl, knew of her?'

'If you think it will help, yes, of course.' Joyce cast her eyes heavenwards again. 'May the Good Lord forgive me.'

Chapter Twenty-nine

'VALERIE....' JOYCE SIGHED, LAPSING FOR SOME MOMENTS INTO A pensive silence. She gave a faint shrug. 'Where does one begin with Valerie? At the beginning, I suppose.'

She looked at Mrs Charles with a faint frown. 'It's a long story and it began, believe it or not, with a film crew arriving in town during that summer, soon after the end of the school year. I can't remember now whether it was a film being made for television or for the big screen – the latter, I am inclined to think, because if it hadn't been for the insistence of the female star in having daily vanloads of freshly arranged flowers delivered to her hotel suite and the caravan she was using while they were filming, I would never have got to know Valerie.'

Joyce turned her head and gazed for a moment at the flowers she had just finished arranging. '*The Sketch*, naturally, got hold of the story and this is what brought Valerie into my shop, asking for a summer job. It was a while before I worked out what she was up to, but eventually I caught on. She was hoping someone important involved in the making of the film and dealing with the demands of the actress for fresh flowers every day, would come into the shop and talent-spot her. Quite frankly, I couldn't see that there was anything all that remarkable about Valerie, but she had other ideas.'

Joyce cast her eyes momentarily heavenwards again and mouthed, '*Forgive me.*'

'She was a pretty enough girl, in a cheap, flashy sort of way,' she went on, 'but I wouldn't have said she had film-star quality, or a chance in a million of becoming an actress, which she told me was her big dream and something she was determined to make happen. There was something decidedly unpleasant about her: she had a real Dr Jekyll and Mrs Hyde personality.' Joyce smiled faintly. 'One minute she could be nice as pie; the next, the exact opposite, although never with me. There was too much at stake: she had to keep on the right side of me or risk being told not to bother coming in. She could be very spiteful and quite cruel; could always find something to laugh at about people behind their backs and sometimes, even to their faces. I thought she enjoyed hurting people and that she particularly liked saying things she knew would upset them. She gave one boy, who came into the shop regularly to see her, and who was absolutely smitten with her, a very hard time of it. Sadly, he committed suicide not long after she died. I don't really know if the two – her death and his suicide – had any bearing on one another, but it crossed my mind at the time that there might have been a connection. She simply didn't give a fig for anybody, and was appallingly rude to her mother, who absolutely doted on her. Her mother took everything Valerie handed out to her without a murmur, almost as if she agreed with the girl that she had every right to say nasty things to her. Her mother worked for a number of families and offices around town as a cleaner and it seemed fairly obvious to me that Valerie was ashamed of her. She called into the shop most days on her way to work to say hello to Valerie, which really got on Valerie's nerves – mine, too, for that matter. Having her skivvy mother around when at any moment, she could be faced with the chance of a lifetime, didn't suit Valerie's image of herself one little bit.'

Joyce fell silent. She gazed for some moments at the flowers lying on the pew beside her before continuing, 'On the plus side, Valerie was a good worker, I won't deny that, but I can't honestly say that I liked her. Among her peers, though, she was definitely very popular, more so with boys – the one I've just mentioned and several others who, like her mother, called in at the shop to see Valerie nearly every day. There was only ever one girlfriend who called in, sometimes on her own, more often than not with those boys—'

'Cheryl Baxter,' guessed Mrs Charles, and Joyce nodded.

'Anyway' – Joyce shrugged – 'as you can imagine, I'd suddenly found myself rushed off my feet, what with my usual orders to deal with as well as the daily needs of the actress, and I was grateful for an extra pair of hands, particularly when it turned out that Valerie had this natural talent for flower arranging. I only had to show her something once and that was it, she could do the job better than I could! The film crew, actors, actresses – the whole kit and caboodle – were here for four or five weeks, from memory, and when they packed up and left, so did Valerie. From my shop, I mean. Overnight she lost interest in everything to do with flowers and actually laughed and said, "*You must be joking!*" when I suggested that she might like to consider becoming a florist when she'd finished her schooling, and that there would be a job waiting for her with me when she left. It wasn't long afterwards that I heard about the accident at the gravel pit and that she was dead. And that is the story of Valerie Ward as I knew her.'

Mrs Charles nodded meditatively. 'There was just one other thing you might be able to help me with,' she said after a moment. 'Would you happen to know the name of the funeral directors whose car turned up at the Baxters' home on the day of the party?'

Joyce nodded. 'Morgan Kempthorne & Sons. I don't think there was any damage to the vehicle, so the Kempthornes didn't press the matter. Not surprisingly, they were as anxious as I was to avoid any adverse publicity.'

After a small pause, Joyce went on, 'Dare I say that I wasn't particularly surprised to hear the rumour that somebody had finally lost it with Valerie and given her a good shove backwards? I would've said it was bound to happen sooner or later. Only a matter of time....'

Joyce remained sitting on the pew in the Lady Chapel for some minutes after Mrs Charles had thanked her and left. Something was bothering her, something she'd said and she couldn't think what it was. *You'll have to remember, Joyce,* she said to herself, *or this will drive you mad.*

Absentmindedly, she picked at the shrivelled petals of a dying Michaelmas daisy.

It suddenly came to her: it was that bit about thinking she'd seen the delivery man, the one who'd paid for the flowers that were delivered to the Baxters, somewhere before. Fair enough, she had seen him before, but it wasn't somewhere round town, it had been there in her shop, but she still couldn't put a name to the face she tried to recall. Her memory was truly shocking, she scolded herself. On reflection, though, having seen a photograph in the paper only yesterday of a man who had been shot by a neighbour over some silly dispute or other, and who, according to what she had read of his murder, was the detective who had investigated Valerie's accident, the one thing she felt she could be fairly confident about now, was that the rumours about his having played a part in the hoax on the Baxters, weren't true. He wasn't the man who had come into her shop and paid for the flowers to be delivered to their home. She would've remembered his face, that shaved head.

Wouldn't she?

She frowned to herself. He might've had some hair back then when Valerie died, but surely he would have been showing signs of going bald. She should still have been able to recognize him from that newspaper photograph, and nothing had rung a bell, not even remotely!

Think again, Joyce. That murdered man definitely isn't the person you are trying to place. You know who it is, too. It's tucked away back there somewhere in your memory....

She felt really frustrated with herself.

He came into the shop regularly, too, didn't he? – collecting flowers that had been ordered.

Not for himself, for someone else. But who?

She felt mildly shocked. That was it, wasn't it? She didn't need to remember the delivery man, his name or what he had looked like: she just had to try and remember who had sent him to collect the flowers on order.

Chapter Thirty

EDWINA CHARLES LOOKED AT THE TIME AND WAS SURPRISED TO SEE how late it had got. She had been sitting for over an hour, ever since her return home from Gidding after having talked to Joyce Cooper, studying the tarot cards in the reading she had given Linda Kellar, and it was now going on for 5.30.

She rose quickly and, as she did so, caught a glimpse through the window of a familiar male figure walking along the road in the direction of her bungalow. She watched him thoughtfully.

David Sayer's eyes were downcast and he gave a start when, a few minutes later, he looked up suddenly and found himself standing on her front porch, facing her.

'Good Lord, I've been out getting a breath of fresh air and I had no idea I'd turned in at your gate!' He grinned self-consciously. 'Although on second thoughts, subconsciously, I was probably looking for a sympathetic ear to hear all my troubles. My aunt again. After I'd left you in Gidding this morning, Jean got a phone call from my aunt's home help. She'd found my aunt collapsed on her living-room floor, and to cut a long story short, Jean and I have moved in with the old girl for a few days. There is apparently no real emergency; in fact, I'm inclined to think the whole business is a put-up job – this was my aunt's way of getting the two of us over here. It's going to be a rough ride. When I sneaked out a short while ago, my aunt was still haranguing Jean for not having put enough salt in the vegetables at lunchtime. I dread to think what's going to be wrong with dinner tonight, and the old girl is sure to find something. I don't know how Jean puts up with it.'

He had followed the clairvoyant into her sitting-room. He glanced at the spread of cards she had been studying. 'Linda Kellar's reading?'

She nodded.

'She's finally turned up,' he said. 'Last night, apparently. She told her brother she'd been walking: that was as much as he could get out of her. That throw any light on your reading?'

Mrs Charles was silent for a moment. Then she said, 'I'm not sure.'

'Well, how about this? I passed on your message to Clive Merton about her having been seen by Stan North getting into Roy Adams's car within a short while of her having left here. Merton immediately arranged for uniform to pay Stan North a visit, and after his version of events was checked out, Linda was taken in and questioned about Roy Adams's shooting.'

Mrs Charles gave him a surprised look.

He gave a faint shrug. 'Roy Adams's neighbour didn't kill him. It's turned into a real puzzler, now that all forensic work has been completed. The shooting has all the signs of having been a professional hit – in all probability, by someone from Adams's days as a copper who's been carrying a grudge around for years. It was a very neat and tidy job by someone who knew exactly what they were doing and how to cover their tracks. Too neat and tidy for it to have been the girl who pulled the trigger.'

They stood side by side gazing down at the cards for some moments, neither speaking. Then David said, 'She's lying, of course ... about what she's been doing.'

'Undoubtedly, but for what she considers to be the best possible reasons,' said Mrs Charles. 'The reading I did for her is very definite. She's covering something up, something she's afraid to bring out into the open for fear that there will be repercussions.'

'I seem to remember your saying something along those lines the last time we discussed her reading.'

'Yes, and the story she's given her brother about her disappearance compounds it. She's desperate that no one should ever find out whatever it is that she's concealing about her mother.'

'And that is? Can't you hazard a guess from her reading?'

Mrs Charles gazed at the cards for a few moments. 'She is either consciously or subconsciously afraid that this knowledge she has about her mother, opens up a distinct possibility that her mother was murdered.'

A faint frown of irritation crossed David's face. 'Are you absolutely sure that this isn't what you want to see? You've always thought Jo Sowerby was murdered, haven't you?'

'I still think it. Jo Sowerby *was* murdered, but I don't know specifically why other than to say that I am convinced that her death is directly linked in some way with what happened to Valerie Ward at the gravel pit all those years ago. Linda doesn't know, either – why her mother might well have been murdered – for now, it is just something she fears, as I've said. I would have seen more in her reading if she knew why someone would want her mother permanently out of the way.' Mrs Charles paused for a moment and looked at David thoughtfully. 'Did Linda deny that she'd been seen with Roy Adams on the day she saw me?'

'No. She said he simply gave her a lift into town. He dropped her off somewhere in the town centre – she'd told him she wanted to do some shopping – and he drove off. After which, according to her, she started walking and didn't stop until she got back home – or rather, turned up at her brother's flat two nights later, asking to borrow his house keys because she'd lost hers, and he drove her home.'

David looked hesitant. 'While we're on the subject … it's all round the village that Stan North had a visit from the police and not surprisingly, with each telling, the reason for their visit has gathered quite a bit of unpleasant moss. I know I shouldn't have said anything to Jean about Stan's having seen the girl, and in normal circumstances, she can be relied upon to keep her counsel. Normal circumstances, however, do not apply to my Aunt Margaret. No one, including Jean and quite often me, is a match for her when she's after some information. She craftily winkled it out of Jean, broadly speaking, what Stan's visit from the boys in blue was all about, and' – he shrugged – 'well, you don't need me to tell you what my aunt is like when it comes to having her say about something. I would lay the larger share of responsibility for the gossip that's going round about the poor chap, squarely at her door. You probably don't need me to tell you that she has never been shy when it comes to voicing her suspicions about the true reason behind his obsession with hedgerows, and now, thanks to her, he has acquired a reputation for being a rampant pervert whose principal occupation, while lurking in the undergrowth, is to leer at young women and think lascivious thoughts about them. This largely because his wife upped and left him many years ago which, according to my aunt, has irreversibly turned his brain.'

Mrs Charles looked concerned. 'I feared something of this nature would happen,' she confessed.

He shrugged. 'Well, what's done is done. As I've said to Jean, he's just going to have to tough it out.'

Mrs Charles recalled the shadow that she had seen in silhouette around Stan's slight frame. 'I'm not so sure that's going to be possible. I've been wondering why I haven't seen him around.'

'There's nothing anybody can do about it now.'

There was a small silence, and then Mrs Charles said, in a pensive voice, 'We'll have to see about that.' She gazed past David for a moment or two, deep in thought. Abruptly, she looked back at him. Her tone became brisk. 'But to get back to Roy Adams. His death does bring things a little more sharply into focus, particularly now that you say his neighbour has been cleared of killing him. The two main protagonists determined to get to the bottom of the Valerie Ward accident are dead: so far as we know, there's nobody now who will stir things up.'

'Except you,' said David wryly.

She smiled faintly. 'Except me.'

That, she thought, *as she stood at the window a few minutes later and watched David walk slowly back to his aunt's cottage, makes it twice now that somebody has done a very neat job of killing somebody and then tidying up after himself.*

Or herself, she amended, with a troubled frown.

Chapter Thirty-one

Linda looked at her watch and flustered colour flooded her cheeks. She quickened her pace. Cheryl had said she'd be bringing round a couple to look at the house at 11.30 and it was almost that now.

Turning the corner into the street where she lived, she breathed a sigh of relief. There was no sign of Cheryl's car and the street was deserted. She hurried up to the front door and let herself in, thankful that she'd taken the time to run the vacuum cleaner over most of the carpets and flicked a duster here and there before slipping out to the convenience store in the next street to get some bread and milk.

She looked at the time again. She probably had less than a minute to put the shopping away. Cheryl would be furious if it were lying about somewhere when she arrived with her prospective buyers. *And we mustn't upset Cheryl!* Linda muttered to herself.

She hurried into the kitchen and was taking a plastic, flavoured milk bottle out of the shopping bag when, with an uncomfortable, prickly feeling creeping up the back of her neck, she sensed that she was not alone in the house. Nervously clutching the bottle to her chest, she looked around quickly over her shoulder. Eddie Nuttall was standing in the kitchen doorway, watching her with an oddly fixed expression on his face.

He walked towards her and instinctively, she took a step backwards away from him.

'Hi,' he said. 'I didn't think anyone was here. I was bringing your keys back: I found them on the dining-room floor after you'd left. They must've fallen out of your shoulder bag. I was just going to leave them here on the kitchen table for you to find when you came in.'

He held out the keys to Linda who, after hesitating momentarily, took them from him.

'Thanks,' she said. Then, 'You'd better go. Cheryl's bringing some people round to look at the house: they'll be here at any moment.'

He made a big show of sniffing under each of his armpits. 'Dear me, and I took a shower before coming out, too.'

It amused him to see Linda change her grip on the milk bottle. She looked as if she were trying to make up her mind whether or not to hit him with it.

'OK, OK, I can take a hint,' he said. 'I'm going.' He turned to leave, almost immediately turning back to her and eyeing her curiously. 'You're scared of Cheryl, aren't you?'

'No, of course not. Why should I be?'

'You tell me.'

'She's just a bit bossy, that's all.'

'Right, and you don't like to upset her.' He nodded his head. 'Very wise.'

The doorbell rang and he grinned. 'Speak of the devil....'

'Please,' said Linda anxiously. 'Do you mind going out the back way?'

He didn't reply; simply brushed past her and did as she had asked.

It was a quick viewing, Cheryl was told by the prospective buyers as they met up with her outside the front of the property, that they didn't like the look of the neighbourhood; it was much too downmarket for their taste. It had also come as a bit of a shock to them to find that there was a cemetery located at such close proximity.

Cheryl was furious, returning to the living-room, where Linda had sat meekly throughout the viewing, and snarling, 'Bloody time wasters. I'm fed up with them! I haven't pulled off a sale in weeks.'

Linda said nothing rather than risk saying the wrong thing. She hoped Cheryl would hurry up and leave. The longer she was there, the more likely it was that she would find something that displeased her.

As if on cue, Cheryl glowered at her. 'I told you we were including all of the white goods in the sale.'

'I remember,' said Linda.

'So please be kind enough, the next time I show people over the house, not to leave soiled linen in the washing machine. I wouldn't have known where to put my face if the last two had wanted to look inside it, and some of them do, you know. They leave no stone unturned.' Cheryl looked at the time. 'I'm running late. I'm supposed to be on the other side of town....'

Linda waited until she heard Cheryl's car driving away, then she went out to the kitchen and stood in front of the washing machine, gazing at it. She could see the waistband of a pair of jeans and what looked like a bundled up grey T-shirt. After a moment, she opened the door of the washing machine and took out the T-shirt. Tiny droplets of what looked like dried blood were spattered over the front of it.

She pushed the T-shirt hurriedly back into the washing machine, almost as if fearful that somebody was watching what she was doing. Her heart was thumping madly; colour flooded her face. *Eddie!* He'd lied about her keys. He'd stolen them, used them to get into the house so that he could leave his bloodstained clothes in the washing machine; hadn't reckoned on her coming back so soon.

She had already reached the conclusion that he'd known of her connection with Roy Adams and that he'd deliberately placed the newspaper report of Roy's shooting where she'd be sure to see it.

She started to shake.

Eddie had also known all along that she'd been with Roy, there at Roy's home, and for all she knew, had even been watching her as she'd handled Roy's shotgun. Eddie was the one who had fired the shot that she'd heard, wasn't he? He killed Roy. *And?* Her brain was momentarily frozen with fear. *And he'd deliberately left his bloodstained clothes where they were sure to incriminate her.*

What other explanation could there be?

She quickly searched in the cupboard under the sink for a black plastic bin liner, frantically rolling up the T-shirt and jeans into a ball and stuffing them into it. She knotted the bag and then hurried out of the house, heading for the towpath alongside the river that flowed through the town.

Chapter Thirty-two

AFTER SLIPPING QUICKLY AWAY THROUGH THE KITCHEN DOOR, EDDIE
Nuttall walked no farther than the corner of the street where he
remained for quite some time, looking back at the house and
waiting.

He saw a couple come out, much too quickly for there being
any chance that they were interested in the property. They drove
off quickly, as if they couldn't shake the dust of that particular
neighbourhood off their shoes fast enough. Five minutes later,
Cheryl Baxter came out and got into her car. He watched her
drive past him. She didn't look his way.

*Would she have recognized him? She hadn't changed; he would
have recognized her anywhere. That scowl on her face, in particular.*

Something hard twisted inside him.

He'd thought with Jo Sowerby and Roy Adams out of the way,
it would be easier.

'*Big mistake,*' he muttered to himself, as Linda Kellar came out
of the house and headed down the street, away from him.

He was going to have to deal with her. It was the last thing he
would have expected, but some sixth sense told him that she was
going to be as big a problem as her mother and Adams. It had
taken a while – in their case, years – but time had eventually
caught up with them and they had both paid the price for their
refusal to leave the past where it was and move on: Jo Sowerby's
daughter wasn't going to be granted the same luxury.

There was something about her body language, her lowered
head and the rigidity of her narrow shoulders, an urgency in her

step, that he found increasingly disturbing. He sensed that it in some way concerned him.

He followed her.

She took the short-cut through the cemetery; he thought she was on her way to the pub where her mother had worked, but then she walked straight past it and then down a narrow side street. This was when he began to think there was a possibility that she was on her way to the river; grew even more puzzled by her intentions when, after walking for some minutes along the towpath, she came to the narrow wooden footbridge that crossed the river where it widened and flowed more swiftly. It appeared to him that she was so deep in thought that she had momentarily lost her bearings, or had forgotten why she was there. She had paused abruptly, looking dazedly all around her. Then moving slowly to one side of the bridge, she gazed down into the muddy, swirling water.

He watched her, convinced that she was going to jump. She continued to gaze down into the river for some minutes and then suddenly she threw the bin liner she had been carrying into it and without a backward glance, turned and walked swiftly along the bridge, retracing her steps.

As she started back in his direction, he ducked behind one of the wooden wild bird hides that were dotted along the towpath. She didn't see him.

Once she was out of sight, he hurried along the towpath to the spot where he thought he remembered seeing the bin liner disappearing into the river. There was no sign of it. The current had carried it away.

He wasn't sure how he felt about that. Linda was another matter. Some people never learn. Her mother hadn't, neither had Adams. Well, so be it. Pay the price, Linda. Pay the price.

Chapter Thirty-three

THE PREMISES OF MORGAN KEMPTHORNE & SONS, FUNERAL Directors, were located down a little used, one-way lane that was tucked away behind the main thoroughfare through Gidding. A double garage, the blue-painted wooden doors to which were closed, was attached to one side of the business.

Mrs Charles had paused for a moment or two to take in the general appearance of her surroundings before entering the building. A familiar, framed reproduction of a pair of hands clasped lightly in prayer was hanging on one wall in Reception. Standing directly beneath it, there was a wooden pedestal on which stood a vase of silk flowers. A Chapel of Rest opened out from the reception area. Both were deserted and fittingly quiet.

There was a small brass handbell standing to one side of a computer on the small desk angled across a corner of the room and, with some trepidation, bearing in mind the complete silence and significance of her surroundings, Mrs Charles carefully picked up the bell and rang it gently.

There was a short wait and then a young, fair-haired man in his late twenties and wearing a dark business suit, came through from the Chapel of Rest with a welcoming smile and an efficient, 'Good morning. How may we help you?'

Mrs Charles returned his greeting. She doubted that he would be the Morgan Kempthorne she hoped to see, and felt fairly certain that this briskly confident young man would be one of the sons. 'I would like to have a word with Mr Morgan Kempthorne, if that is possible, please.'

'Mrs Morgan Kempthorne, my mother,' he corrected Mrs

Charles pleasantly. 'Yes, certainly.' He lifted the receiver on the phone on the desk and pressed a button, after a moment explaining to the person at the other end of the line that Mrs Kempthorne was wanted in Reception.

Morgan Kempthorne was a well-built woman, unusually tall for her sex at six feet one inch in height, with fading brown hair drawn back from her face in a neat French pleat. But for a dark, downy moustache, she would have been quite handsome. She was in her early fifties and was dressed smartly, like her son, in a dark business suit.

She shook hands with Mrs Charles and said, 'Morgan Kempthorne.' And then, in an echo of the remainder of her son's greeting, and in a solicitous, rather more practised voice, 'How may we help you, my lovely?'

Morgan Kempthorne moved to take a seat behind the desk and indicated to the chair in front of it for Mrs Charles to do likewise.

Mrs Charles introduced herself and then followed much the same line of approach she had adopted when approaching Joyce Cooper about the events that had taken place at the Baxters' children's party.

As she explained the reasons behind her need for this information, Mrs Charles watched the other woman's grey eyes become guarded. Her response to Mrs Charles's revelation that she was a clairvoyant, was faintly patronizing. 'I would have thought that in the circumstances – as this young woman, you say, is so seriously disturbed – a psychiatrist or a psychologist would have been a more appropriate professional to approach with the problem of her nightmares.'

'That's as may be,' said Mrs Charles imperturbably, 'she nevertheless chose to come to me for help, or rather, it was her late mother' – Mrs Charles hesitated slightly – 'Josephine Sowerby, who had attended the Baxters' children's party with her, who sent her to me.'

Morgan Kempthorne's neatly shaped eyebrows rose a fraction, but she made no comment.

'Did you ever discover who borrowed the funeral car that arrived at the children's party?' asked Mrs Charles.

'Is this somehow relevant to the young woman's nightmares?' enquired Morgan Kempthorne coolly.

'Only in so far as I am personally convinced that in all probability, she subconsciously fears that she knows who took it and that the same person used it, quite deliberately, in conjunction with the floral tributes that were delivered to the Baxters' home during the afternoon of the party.' Mrs Charles paused; watched Morgan Kempthorne's eyes closely as she continued, 'Her nightmares stem, in my opinion, from her fear that her mother organized the delivery of flowers that day. Wouldn't you agree, then, that this raises the further possibility of her mother having had a hand in the unauthorized use of your funeral car?'

There was a faint edge to the funeral director's voice as she responded. 'Well, my lovely, that makes a very interesting theory; I am only sorry that there is very little I can tell you that would confirm it one way or the other. The night before the vehicle in question was purloined by a person or persons unknown, it was left parked further down the lane outside these premises while our garage was undergoing some major alterations. There are no parking restrictions between the hours of six and nine in this part of town, and when I arrived here soon after nine-thirty the following morning and there was no sign of the vehicle, I assumed that one of my sons had moved it elsewhere for the day. I never gave the matter another thought until a police officer arrived late in the afternoon and asked me if we were missing one of our funeral cars. If so, it could be collected from – and he gave me an address which turned out to be the Baxters'. I sent my sons straight round there to collect it. We had no idea then who had taken it and, presumably, gone for a joyride in it, and I and my sons are none the wiser today. The police had no idea who'd taken it, either.'

'This was how you were prepared to accept things? That someone had taken the vehicle for a joyride – despite floral tributes having been left at the Baxters' home at or around the same time?'

'These things happen; they are a nuisance,' said Morgan Kempthorne in an even voice, 'no damage was done to the vehicle; my sons returned it here in the same condition that it had been left the previous evening when one of them had parked it in the lane, and that was all I cared about. I certainly didn't want the police wasting their precious time running all over the place and making a big fuss about something that, fortunately, so far as we were concerned, wounded our pride in ourselves and the quality of the service we offer the bereaved of Gidding, and caused us, as I'm sure you will appreciate, not some little embarrassment. The kind of publicity this sort of thing would generate is most inappropriate to our particular line of business. We couldn't afford to have bereaved families bypass us because they feared we were so negligent with our vehicles that their dear departed ran the risk of being transported by some thrill-seeking young pranksters all around town. The sooner the matter was forgotten, the better.'

Morgan Kempthorne looked at her watch and rose to her feet. 'I'm sorry, we have a funeral this morning. I'm afraid you will have to excuse me.'

Mrs Charles stood up. 'Thank you for your time.' She turned as if to leave; paused. 'There was just one other thing: did you know Josephine Sowerby?'

'I read what happened to her in the cemetery.' The funeral director's eyebrows went up. 'It is that Josephine Sowerby you are referring to, isn't it? She suffered a fatal heart attack, I believe. That's all I know about the poor woman, what I read in the paper. We haven't seen her here, if that's what you mean.'

Mrs Charles made no comment, thanked her again and turned and left.

Morgan Kempthorne's son was waiting for his mother, blocking her passage through the Chapel of Rest.

She looked at him with cold eyes. 'You heard?' she asked him.

He gave a small snort of disgust. 'And so the chickens come home to roost.'

'I hardly think so.'

'You know who she is, don't you?'

'That charlatan? I thought the silly season and all those who partake of it were something others had to put up with, not us.'

'That charlatan, Mother dear, if you'd been listening properly when she introduced herself, is Edwina Charles, and from what I've read of Edwina Charles, the clairvoyant,' he added, with heavy emphasis on the words *the clairvoyant* and giving his mother a steely look, 'she doesn't go round asking questions for the fun of it, and she doesn't suffer fools gladly which, I'd say, puts you right in the frame. That was no casual enquiry she made about you and Jo Sowerby. To put it more succinctly, Mother dear, I am picking up some very strong paranormal vibrations of my own that Jo Sowerby didn't die of natural causes; she was murdered, and that this is really what's giving her kid nightmares.'

'That's supposed to give me disturbed nights, too, is it?'

'It would me.' *Mother dear*, he added under his breath.

Chapter Thirty-four

LINDA SAT ON HER BED, HUGGING HER KNEES TIGHTLY TO HER CHEST. One thought kept chasing itself round in her head: she had to get away, go someplace where nobody knew anything about her and her crazy family. *But where? When? Before the wedding? After the wedding? Is there even going to be a wedding? Barry's bored rigid with all of it, she could see it in his eyes. Cheryl has got to be an absolute pain; always was, but this past week or so she's been ten times worse.*

How could Cheryl change so quickly and go from being somebody who used to be a bit like me, thought Linda, and managed to keep well in the background, to being the person she'd become lately, so bossy and irritable all the time?

Maybe it really was the stress of all the wedding arrangements: Barry certainly wasn't much help with them, though the way Cheryl was behaving, no one could blame him. The slightest thing and Cheryl bit his head off.

No, there was more to it with Cheryl.

Since Mum died....

That was when Cheryl changed, wasn't it? She'd been so afraid of Mum – truth be told, all three of them had, Barry, Cheryl and I – Linda admitted to herself, with a small frown.

Her thoughts drifted back over the years.

For as far back as she could remember, her mother had always been unpredictable, no doubt thanks to her heavy drinking which had made it impossible to be sure of her mood. It had always been wise to tread very softly around her, speaking only when spoken to, and then choosing every word that was uttered with utmost care. Sometimes it was the most innocent of remarks that would set her off and then she could be quite violent ... smashing things up – anything she could lay her hands on, once she got mad about something. She never hit us – Barry and me – though, Linda reminded herself: Sowerby was the only one she actually attacked physically when she was drunk. That was probably why he left. He was a horrible man, Linda recalled with a shudder. But perhaps even that was her mother's fault.

Linda lay back against her pillows and then, placing her hands behind her head, she gazed up at the ceiling.

If they gave out prizes for dysfunctional families, she thought miserably, it would have been blue ribbons all round for the Kellar/Sowerby family. She couldn't honestly hold out hope for any change there in the future, either. Her mother's shadow was always going to hang over them; it was going to be as if she'd never gone from their lives. And all because of something that happened years ago which her mother simply couldn't let go of. Some kind of accident.... Her mother had never spoken of it to her, it was just that thing, that something terrible that had happened that had driven her to drink more heavily than ever before and had brought that dreadful Roy Adams into their lives. Linda had often thought that Cheryl – Barry, too, for that matter – knew what was behind her mother's drinking and unpredictable mood swings, but she, Linda, hadn't wanted to know, didn't want to know now, just wanted to get away from all of them. Eddie, too.

She leaned forward and hugged her knees again, pressing her forehead hard on to them.

Why would Eddie have wanted to kill Roy Adams? Why had he wanted to push the blame for his murder on to her by leaving his bloodstained clothes where somebody was bound to find them eventually?

She'd never done anything to him, she thought bitterly. Until two weeks ago, she'd never even heard of Eddie Nuttall!

She'd caught him out, hadn't she? Leaving those things in the washing machine had only been part of it. She'd returned home too quickly, before he'd had time to finish what he'd planned for her. It was a stroke of luck that Cheryl had turned up with those people when she had.

A sudden chill settled across Linda's shoulders. She didn't really want to go there, think about any of this. But now that she'd started, she couldn't hold any of it back.

This had something to do with her mother, didn't it? Was it some kind of vendetta against her and Roy Adams? Roy hadn't touched alcohol, not so far as Linda was aware – she'd certainly never seen him worse for drink, anyway – but in his own way, he'd been just as crazy as her mother was.

She started to tremble again.

What was she thinking? she asked herself. *That Eddie killed them, both of them? Roy Adams, yes ... that looked pretty definite. But her mother, too?*

It would explain one thing: the mistake that was made at the cemetery. Linda didn't know what this mistake meant, she only knew that one had been made and that it could change everything.

This was something she wasn't going to think about. Her mother had died of a heart attack, there was no mistake about that. *And let's be serious about this,* Linda said to herself, *what on earth could Eddie Nuttall have had to do with her mother – Roy Adams, too, for that matter? Why on earth would he want to kill them, that was what it all boiled down to, wasn't it?*

The accident.... Was that what connected him to them?

What else could it be?

Chapter Thirty-five

As David Sayer spoke her name in greeting, Edwina Charles was stooping to gather up some leaves that due to the abnormally wet summer, had been shed early by a weeping silver birch. He was leaning on her front gate; had been watching her for some minutes, reluctant to interrupt her at her work.

'Sorry if I startled you,' he apologized when she looked up at him quickly. He opened the gate and walked over to her as she straightened up. 'I've been wondering if there have been any developments.... Linda Kellar,' he explained, when she looked at him quizzically. 'Did she get back in touch with you?'

'No. There has only ever been a very slight possibility of that which decreases with the passing of each day, unfortunately. But there has been one small development,' Mrs Charles admitted. She smiled to herself. 'That's if you're interested.'

He grinned. 'OK, so I've not been with you a hundred per cent on this one, but I'm always open and willing to listen to anything that might make me change my mind.'

'I deliberately came out here this evening to catch up on some tidying up in the garden to try and clear my thoughts,' she confessed.

'Has it worked?'

'Up to a point. I spoke to Mrs Kempthorne this morning – the Gidding funeral director whose car was taken and driven to the Baxters' children's party,' Mrs Charles added when David looked at her blankly.

'Oh yes, the lady with a name I've always thought was a boy's,' David said with a quick nod. 'Something of an Amazon to look at, isn't she? Very impressive, though I've only seen her on one occasion, at the funeral of a close friend several years ago.'

'She knows who took the car.'

'She's admitted this?' He paused. 'Merton said she asked the police to stand down and not take any further steps in the matter.'

'Which she mentioned to me and confirms my suspicions.'

'Ah.' He gave his head a slow nod. 'So this is just one of your special insights: she hasn't actually admitted anything.'

'She won't, either. And in the circumstances, that could prove to be no bad thing, but only provided she doesn't contact whoever took the car and tell that person I went to see her this morning.'

He looked at her in surprise. 'What are you saying? That she's next in the firing line?'

'Let's just say Morgan Kempthorne would be taking a very serious risk if she doesn't take the advice she gave the police and stand down and then step well back from the person or persons who took the car.' Mrs Charles gazed past David and he watched her eyes darken perceptibly, a foreboding, which he had come to recognize, of something that very possibly would soon come to pass. 'There is unfinished business here.' She looked back at David suddenly. 'That is what this is all about, Superintendent. Unfinished business.'

Chapter Thirty-six

CHERYL WATCHED BARRY WITH INCREASING FRUSTRATION. HE HAD been reading a scientific medical journal ever since they had finished dinner; said there was nothing interesting on television, but she could watch it if she wanted to, it wouldn't disturb him.

She was so steamed up about what she considered to be her second lost sale of the day that watching television was the last thing she wanted to do. She wanted to tell him about her day and, as the minutes passed, and the silence in the room grew heavier, she couldn't contain herself for a moment longer. She spoke angrily, didn't mean to, it was just the way it came out.

'I've had a terrible day: I lost another sale this afternoon.'

'I can't say my day was much better,' he said. Realizing that his reading was probably at an end for the night, that Cheryl was determined to have a conversation, he closed the journal and put it aside.

'That's all I seem to get these days, time wasters,' she went on.

He nodded. Wasn't really listening: his thoughts had drifted back to the article he had been reading on what was alleged to be a significant advancement in the treatment of infertile women with a history of repeated failure with IVF. It all seemed pie in the sky to him, more wishful thinking on the part of the scientist carrying out the research, but it made interesting reading nonetheless.

'Are you listening to me?' she asked him after a moment. Her tone was challenging; he decided to pay proper attention rather than risk another night of her sulking because things weren't just as Cheryl wanted.

'Yes,' he said. Then, in a direct contradiction of this assurance: 'What did you say?'

'I said it's time you had a word with Linda about clearing out your mother's things and taking them to one of the charity shops in town. I've never felt so embarrassed. The couple I showed over the house this morning looked in your mother's wardrobe and even from where I was standing, way back in the doorway, I could smell the stench of booze that wafted out. It was disgusting.'

He looked at her. 'Did they ask your permission to open the wardrobe?'

'You must be joking! No more than any of them ask if it's OK to check inside the oven to see if it's clean. They've probably not once cleaned their own oven this side of last Christmas, but that's different. Everybody else's oven has to be spotless!'

He seemed intrigued by this anomaly; thought about it for a moment and then he said, 'I don't think it's such a good idea to give Mum's clothes away to anyone if they stink that much. But I'll get Linda to go through everything and bundle it all up into bin liners for me to take to the tip.'

'The sooner the better.'

'Consider it done.'

'Have you thought about the funeral?'

The sudden change of subject took him by surprise and he looked at her for a moment, as if trying to think whose funeral it was that he should be arranging. Then he asked, 'In what way?'

She hesitated momentarily before replying. 'Well, there isn't a problem, is there?'

'What do you mean?'

'With the police.'

'Not so far as I know.'

'But you haven't actually been told officially that you can go ahead and arrange your mother's funeral, have you?'

'All in good time. There's probably so much paperwork involved, they keep putting it off. What's the rush, anyway? I thought we'd decided it would be better to hold off on the funeral until after we were married.'

Cheryl frowned. 'It's just that....'

He curbed the flash of impatience that went through him when she didn't finish. *What now?* he asked himself wearily.

'I think I saw somebody today,' she said after a moment.

'What do you mean by *somebody*? Somebody special? The Queen, David Beckham – who?'

Barry waited for her to get angry with him for being flippant and was surprised when she said, quite simply, 'I'm not sure. This man was standing on the corner of the street when I drove away from your mother's home this morning.' She hesitated. 'From a distance, it certainly looked like it might have been him. He was staring at the house – I'm sure he was, Barry. I only caught a quick glimpse of him; there was a lot of traffic about and I was concentrating on that, and it wasn't until I'd driven on a bit further that I began to wonder if I'd been seeing things. As soon as I could, I turned round and went back to make sure, but he'd gone.'

'Who'd gone?'

'Him. The man I'd seen standing on the corner. It was Andrew Tomlinson; I'm positive it was him.'

'Rubbish. What would he be doing back here?'

'Some people do come home, Barry. Not everybody finds wall-to-wall sunshine and barbies their cup of tea. He's back, Barry. I know it was him.'

'I thought people emigrated to Australia for sun, sand, sea and barbecues, not New Zealand,' remarked Barry. 'That was where Tomlinson and his family went after they'd left here, wasn't it?'

'Australia, New Zealand, what difference does it make?' She spoke impatiently.

'Ask an Aussie or Kiwi that question and see what sort of an answer you get,' he replied drily. 'Anyway, so what! He's back. Big deal.'

'He's following me, Barry.'

'Now you're being paranoid. Besides, he'd need to be pretty athletic to keep up with you.' He grinned. 'You said he was standing on the corner, so I'm assuming he was on foot.'

'I'm being serious about this. You know what he said to me: he swore he'd get me for what I did to Valerie.'

Barry sighed. 'He was a fourteen-year-old kid, Cheryl. We all were … just kids. Besides, you did nothing to Valerie except give her a little push and now that he's grown up and had time to think things over – that's if he ever thinks about it, which I very much doubt – he'd know that. Probably wouldn't even remember what he'd said to you. I'm sorry to say this to you, Cheryl, but you're getting to be as bad as Mum and Roy Adams were about Valerie. For God's sake let go and move on.'

Cheryl was shaking her head. 'You know your trouble, don't you? You live in cloud cuckoo land.'

'And very pleasant it is here, too, Cheryl. You should try it sometime.'

Chapter Thirty-seven

CHERYL SAT ALONE IN THE LIVING-ROOM, HER HEAD RESTING BACK against the sofa and her eyes closed. Barry had gone to bed something like two hours ago, but she knew that if she followed him, she would never be able to get to sleep. There was too much on her mind.

She had a terrible headache: she'd been getting a lot of headaches lately, but this one, since seeing Andrew Tomlinson today, was by far the worst.

It *was* Andrew Tomlinson. He'd been in a car accident as a small child and had suffered a badly injured shoulder which had needed surgery, after which he had always stood with a slight lean to the left. The man standing on the corner today had had the same tendency to lean to the left which most people wouldn't notice, but which she would never forget, principally because she had always feared this day, that Andrew had meant what he'd said and that he'd come back one day and carry out his threat. Of them all, he had been the strong one, the peacemaker.

She had tried so often lately to picture Valerie's face, what had been so special about it that Andrew, that terrible wimp, Bernard Watson, and yes, even Barry, despite his denials, had followed her round like lost little poodle puppy-dogs, but her features had become a blur. She could only remember Valerie's voice, she heard it most nights in her sleep, screeching at her as she slipped down the side of the gravel pit and disappeared from sight.

Jo had thought she was so clever in giving in without a fight when Barry had told her that they had been seeing one another for a very long time and were in love and wanted to get married.

She had seen it as her best chance, after all the years of insinuation and constant pressure on anybody and everybody, no matter how remotely connected with what had happened to Valerie, of getting the confession she had wanted.

Poor deluded Jo.

Poor deluded Barry! He couldn't see it, could he? It should have been the end of it, she'd honestly thought it was when Jo died, but then Roy Adams was shot, and that changed everything. She was sure then that it was never going to be over. There might have been hope if it had been a neighbour-from-hell-shooting the way everybody had thought initially, but now the papers were saying that the police were looking for someone else for his murder, someone from his past with a grudge against him, and that meant they would take a much closer look at every investigation that he had ever been involved in as a police officer, including Valerie's death. Maybe this was what Andrew Tomlinson was doing back here: the police had sent for him because they wanted to go back over his witness statement with him.

If she confessed to killing Valerie would that be the finish of it? She had often thought about it, confessing, but hadn't been sure what would happen to her. She wasn't sure now. What if it meant her having to go to prison? She'd probably have to serve some time in prison, even though it was all a long while ago. Would Barry stand by her if she confessed? He kept saying she should let go and move on, but what about him, would he let go and move on? Hadn't she suffered enough? she asked herself bitterly. What she and her family had had to go through all these years, hounded by Jo and Roy Adams and all the innuendo, had been far worse than serving a prison sentence. She wished they had charged her at the time and been done with it. It would all be behind her whereas now it was all in front of her ... now when there was so much more at stake.

She would take a chance on confessing if she could be sure of the outcome, that she wouldn't lose Barry and be faced with only a suspended sentence or with having to serve a period of time doing community service. She wished there was someone she could ask, someone who could advise her as to what would be the best way forward.

She considered this for some minutes; found her thoughts drifting on to Linda and the clairvoyant she had gone to.

It might be an answer. She had to talk to someone about this or she would go mad.

There was no need to mention Valerie....

She could give a false name, simply say she was concerned about her future prospects and needed help in deciding what would be the best thing to do ... see what the clairvoyant would come up with.

Cheryl wished she could ask Linda exactly what the clairvoyant – a Mrs Charles, Cheryl seemed to remember that newspaper reporter having mentioned to her – had said to her, but that could prove risky. Linda might tell Barry that she was thinking of consulting her and he would want to know why. She would want to hear what the clairvoyant had to say first.

Cheryl sighed to herself. It was just a thought, a crazy one at that. She probably wouldn't do anything about it.

Chapter Thirty-eight

CYRIL SAT ON EDWINA CHARLES'S SOFA IN HER SITTING-ROOM, gripping his knees tightly in his hands and staring straight ahead. He had been sitting like this ever since arriving at her home twenty minutes earlier, and since when he hadn't uttered a sound. His sister sat with him and waited patiently. He had called for a reason, and when he had sorted out his thinking, he would tell her what that was.

'He's in a bad way,' he said finally. He glared at Mrs Charles accusingly.

'I'm sorry, Cyril,' she said. Then, after a small pause, 'I wasn't paying attention and I missed the first part of what you said.'

'Stan North, of course,' he replied sharply.

'Oh,' she said with a small nod. 'I assume you are referring to the gossip surrounding the visit he had from the police in connection with that missing young girl, and the part I played in it. Well, Cyril, I am truly sorry about that, and I very much regret that Mr North found it necessary to take me into his confidence, because in so doing, he placed me in a position where, if he didn't go to the police, I would become culpable for withholding vital evidence that could have led to the discovery of the whereabouts of the girl.'

'They found her, didn't they? I don't see why you had to drag him into it.' Cyril's tone was piqued which Mrs Charles found perfectly understandable. Cyril and Stan were kindred spirits, both living similar lives in their own, exclusive little worlds.

'I believe so, though at the time of my speaking to David Sayer about what Stan had seen, it hadn't been made public that she had returned to her home unharmed,' she explained.

'I had to stop a couple of youngsters from throwing stones at the windows of his house yesterday afternoon. A good clip around the ears, is what they need.'

'I certainly hope you didn't give them one apiece,' said Mrs Charles. 'You could find yourself in quite serious trouble.'

Cyril gave her a baleful look. He made no comment.

They lapsed into another silence, both remaining seated. Mrs Charles was sure there was more her brother had to say to her.

'He won't leave his home,' said Cyril after a few minutes. 'Everybody's giving him cold looks and whispering terrible things behind his back about his wife having left him and taking their daughter with her.'

'I know,' she replied quietly. There was a small pause, and then she added, 'Try not to let this upset you too much, Cyril. These things have a way of righting themselves.'

There was another long silence and then Cyril said, simply, 'I said no.'

Mrs Charles waited. He said no more. 'No, to what?' she asked him.

He stared hard at her, as if seeing her for the first time in his life. 'Joyce Cooper ... she asked me to consider rejoining the cathedral choir.'

He stood up, glared at his sister and then walked out. He was back ten minutes later.

'You are not to discuss this with her over the phone,' he warned his sister.

Mrs Charles considered for a moment. 'Please forgive me, Cyril, but we are talking about your rejoining the choir, aren't we?'

'That, too,' he said.

Mrs Charles waited.

'When you go to see her,' he said.

'I see,' she said in a thoughtful voice. Then, 'When would this be, Cyril?'

'Joyce said any day but a Wednesday.'

Finally, thought Mrs Charles with a small sigh, Cyril had got round to telling her why he had called in the first place. 'Thank you, Cyril,' she said meekly.

Mrs Charles walked up to Stan North's shabby front door and knocked on it. There being neither a knocker nor a bell push, she used her bare knuckles, dislodging more of the door's black, flaking paintwork.

There was no immediate response from within and then, after knocking once more and a wait of the best part of two minutes, she heard a few shuffling footsteps. Nothing happened for a moment and then the door opened, but only a mere crack.

'Good morning, Mr North,' said Mrs Charles. She spoke cheerfully, despite being appalled by the glimpse she was given of the man's unshaven features and sickly grey pallor. The brown tartan dressing-gown he was wearing was tied loosely at the waist. It was clean, but bearing in mind the lateness of the morning and the fact that he hadn't bothered to dress properly, it gave him an overall dishevelled appearance. 'I'm so pleased to have found you in,' she went on. 'I need your advice about a woolly bear ... at least, I am assuming that it was a woolly bear I spotted in my garden this morning. I've been doing a lot of clearing up outside, and I am particularly anxious not to dig up any of the herbaceous plants woolly bears feed on. Perhaps you could advise me.'

The door opened a little wider. 'You mean the caterpillar of *Arctia caja*, the Garden Tiger Moth,' he said, a glimmer of interest creeping into his lifelessly dull, hazel eyes.

'Yes, of course,' she said with a quick laugh. 'I'm sorry, I should've said. As a child, I, and many of my young friends, always called Garden Tiger Caterpillars woolly bears.'

'I did, too,' he admitted with a slow nod.

'I am aware that this species of moth has declined in many places in recent years and I naturally wish to do everything I can to ensure that the woolly bear I'm almost certain I've seen, will duly metamorphose into a beautiful Garden Tiger.'

She could see Stan was interested. It might have been a trick of the light, but she would have sworn that she could see healthy colour coming back into his cheeks. 'This is exciting news, Mrs Charles: it's been a long time since I've seen either a woolly bear or a Garden Tiger Moth,' he confessed. 'I'll be over in a little while and you can show me the plants you were thinking of digging up.'

'That is very kind of you, Mr North,' she responded. 'I am obliged to you. I look forward to seeing you.'

Mrs Charles walked back towards her home, offering up a small prayer asking for forgiveness, and giving as her only defence for the deception she had just perpetrated on Stan North in regard to her having sighted a Garden Tiger Caterpillar, that it was in a good cause.

She was pleased to see her near neighbours, Edna and Philip Dixon, working in their front garden as she drew level with their home.

They exchanged greetings and then, determinedly ignoring a niggling qualm over her intention of using the Dixons to compound her deception, Mrs Charles said, 'Stan North and I are on the trail of a woolly bear caterpillar. At least, we will be when he calls on me in a short while. I don't know if you're familiar with this caterpillar, but I have an idea that I might have seen one feeding in my garden.'

Philip was nodding his head. 'It turns into a moth, doesn't it? I remember it from when I was a youngster. I haven't seen one in years.'

'I thought—' Edna began. She broke off, looking vaguely embarrassed. 'Well, we haven't seen Mr North about for a day or two. I mean, there's never a day goes by that you don't see him somewhere around the village, is there? And there's been all that unpleasant talk about him. We thought he might've gone away.'

'Good heavens, no!' Mrs Charles contrived to look extremely surprised by the suggestion. 'Why on earth would he want to go away at this time of year when the insect life in the hedgerows is at its busiest? As for the gossip surrounding him concerning the visit he received from the police, the information he was able to give them about his having seen that missing young girl walking along this road, was a great help to them. They are extremely grateful to him. Anyway, what I particularly wanted to say to you is that Mr North and I would be very pleased if you would keep an eye out for these caterpillars. It would also be a great help to us and the moth society if you'd make a point of alerting all the gardening enthusiasts you can think of living in and around the village, as to our interest in them. The more of us keeping a close watch for them, the merrier!'

'Indeed we will,' Philip assured her earnestly. 'Our planet is in crisis: we should all do our part to protect and preserve what we've got for as long as possible. I've often said to Edna that Stan North's doing all of us a sterling service, working as he does keeping tabs on our hedgerows.'

Edna shot him a mildly surprised look, but she made no comment.

Mrs Charles thanked them both and walked on. Job done. Or one, hopefully, making a start in the right direction, she thought with a little sigh.

Chapter Thirty-nine

LINDA KELLAR BREATHED IN DEEPLY AND THEN EXHALED SLOWLY. She had bagged up the clothing – underwear, mostly – she had taken from the chest of drawers standing to one side of her mother's bedroom window, which only left the single drawer in the dressing-table and the wardrobe to be emptied. Cheryl had called in just under an hour ago with a bundle of black plastic bin liners for her to fill, and had warned her that she would be back later to collect them. Linda was finding the job unpleasant and distressing, and flopping down on the bed, asked herself if all this rush to get rid of her mother's things was really necessary. She could understand Cheryl's argument, what didn't reek of alcohol was permeated with passive cigarette smoke from the pub where her mother used to work, but if it bothered Cheryl that much, why didn't she do this job herself? Linda was quite sure that Cheryl would find fault with what she was doing: nobody these days, not even Barry, could do anything right in Cheryl's eyes.

Linda snorted softly through her nose. Cheryl probably thought that clearing the house of all these intimate personal items and their distinctive odours would also help free her of the spectre of her fiancé's mother, but there was no chance of that happening. If Cheryl and Barry couldn't see it, Linda certainly could. Things had got worse for Cheryl since their mother had died. This mysterious hold their mother had always seemed to have over Cheryl, had grown even stronger during the past week. Linda recalled the night that Barry had driven her home after she had mislaid her keys, and the comment she had made to him that she thought Cheryl was close to losing it. He had merely expressed surprise, claiming not to have noticed any major change in her conduct. He had admitted that Cheryl was, perhaps, a little edgier than usual; they all were: the wedding arrangements, on top of everything else, were getting them all down.

Linda reflected on this for a moment: then, rising and crossing to the wardrobe to make a start there, she sighed and said, out loud, 'No, Barry. It isn't the wedding: Cheryl's worked too hard to get you up the aisle for it to be that. Get your head out of those crossword puzzles you're addicted to and take a good look around you for a change....'

She opened the wardrobe, freed a calf-length, grubby, beige suede jacket, a heavy, black wool topcoat and a duffel jacket that she hadn't seen her mother wearing in years, from their hangers and then dumped them in a pile on the bed. The suede jacket slithered on to the floor. As she picked it up, she automatically checked the inside pocket to make sure that it was empty. Her fingers closed around something stiff and papery and she withdrew it curiously. It was a photograph.

The hand holding it began to shake. The face of the man who smiled up at her from the glossy print belonged to Eddie Nuttall.

Her eyes watered with the strain of looking at his smiling face and she blinked several times to clear her vision.

Turning the photograph over, she read what was written on the back of it. *Me and my little sister Marama, taken two years ago on an Auckland beach not far from our home. Sorry I haven't anything more recent, but I don't think I've changed much; you should be able to recognize me.* A signature had been scrawled beneath this message. It wasn't the name Linda had expected to see and her brow furrowed as she read it. *Andrew.*

Andrew?

Linda's frown deepened. She couldn't make any sense of the photograph and the message on the back of it in relation to her mother, other than to think that this man she knew as Eddie and her mother had arranged to meet. *But where, when?* At sometime in the future? Or had they already met before her mother died? And why did they meet, or plan to meet?

She sat down on the foot of the bed and stared at the photograph.

Eddie, whose real name was probably Andrew, knew Roy Adams and obviously knew her mother....

Both of whom were now dead.

It was a sudden thought that came into Linda's head and it chilled her to the bone. She couldn't see the connection there must have been between Eddie and her mother, but she knew there definitely had to be one buried somewhere in her mother's past. Barry might know what this was, but she certainly didn't, and that could only mean it was something that had happened a long time ago. She couldn't recall her mother ever having mentioned anybody by the name of Andrew.

Linda bit anxiously into her bottom lip. She hadn't wanted Barry to know anything about her and Eddie – Barry had enough to worry about right now – but she was going to have to show him this photograph, wasn't she? She could no longer keep any of this to herself. She had to face facts. Eddie, or whatever his real name was, had had a long-standing connection with their mother, who had agreed to meet him.

In the cemetery – to try and sort something out between them?

She frowned thoughtfully to herself. It would fit, wouldn't it? Be one explanation for the mistake the police had made about where her mother was attacked ... and it was a mistake.

She thought about this for a moment. Eddie was someone else who had made a mistake, wasn't he? He had attacked her mother somewhere in the cemetery, causing the injuries to her head – which he might have thought had killed her – and then for some reason, he had carried her from the spot where the attack had taken place and left her in the wrong place. That was what it amounted to, wasn't it? Her mother had been left by him for dead in the wrong place because he'd had no idea that she never went anywhere near that part of the cemetery.

Linda closed her eyes for a moment, struggling to arrange her thoughts in some sort of order. The best that she could come up with was that Eddie had arranged to meet her mother for the sole purpose of killing her, providing her beforehand with a photograph of himself so that she would recognize him. Then, after he had killed her, he had arranged to meet Roy at Roy's home for the sole purpose of killing him, too.

A sharp stab of shock went through Linda.

The connection between her mother and Roy had always been the one thing, that girl who had died, which could only mean that Eddie was somehow involved in what had happened to her.

It was the only thing that made sense.

Chapter forty

CHERYL LOADED THE LAST OF SIX BIN LINERS INTO THE BOOT OF HER car and then leaned forward over the final one and pressed down heavily on it with both hands, expelling some of the air in it which had made it bulkier than the others. She remained like this for some moments, eyes closed. *What next?* she asked herself.

Linda had said that she was coming over to the flat tonight to see Barry; it was urgent, she'd said. She wouldn't say what it was all about, but she was white as a ghost. Cheryl couldn't quite explain why she was so sure of this, but she had sensed instinctively that Linda's mysterious boyfriend, Eddie, had something to do with this urgent need of hers to see her brother. It was all so secretive; had been all along: first Linda's friendship with him, and now this, thought Cheryl irritably. Linda must think she was thick if she couldn't guess what was going on. The selfish little bitch was going to tell Barry that she was pregnant, wasn't she? Well, tough luck. She'd have to hold her horses on that one. Tonight was right out of the question. She and Barry were having dinner with friends – in fact, she was running late, would have to get a move on – and Barry was attending a conference in Leeds over the weekend. He and one of his work colleagues were leaving straight from the hospital tomorrow night as soon as they had finished up for the day. It would have to be Monday night: Linda could wait that long to put another spoke in the wheel of their wedding plans, couldn't she?

Cheryl's expression soured. The girl didn't even have the decency to wait until after the wedding to break the happy news to Barry. Not that it *was* happy news; anything but, in her opinion. Linda had looked sick and had actually been in the toilet throwing up when Cheryl had arrived to collect the bin bags to take to the rubbish tip on her way home from the agency.

Cheryl straightened up, drew back from the boot and then slammed down the lid. She turned with a sharp intake of breath; hadn't realized that a young man waited on the footpath to speak to her. She stood perfectly still, staring at him. Her heart was pumping so hard it was painful.

It was a moment or two before she found her voice.

'Andrew? It is Andrew, isn't it?' She took an involuntary step away from him as she spoke.

'Long time no see, Cheryl,' he replied.

Chapter forty-one

HAVING HEARD A CAR DRAWING UP OUTSIDE HER BUNGALOW, MRS Charles left Stan North to pick up where he had left off the previous day in his search for the woolly bear caterpillar that, with the very best of intentions, she had falsely claimed to have seen in her garden. He was given her solemn assurance that she would return to discuss his findings, if any, as soon as her client had left.

She ushered Cheryl Baxter into her sitting-room, joining her there some minutes later with a tea tray. It was a procedure that she purposefully adopted with a prospective new client to give that person time to collect his or her thoughts and begin to relax.

As she poured tea for them both, the clairvoyant said, 'When you telephoned me yesterday, you explained that you are concerned for' – she hesitated briefly – 'I believe you said it was the sister of the man you are to marry in a few weeks' time. I confess that I am a little puzzled that you should think I would be able to be of any assistance to you personally over these concerns of yours, presumably for her well-being.'

'I'm sorry,' said Cheryl. 'I intended to say more when we spoke, but while I was still on the phone to you, Barry, my fiancé, came home and I thought it best if I talked to you first about my worries concerning his sister. Particularly since she and my fiancé have only recently lost their mother. She told him that she came to see you because their late mother, Josephine Sowerby, felt she needed help in deciding her future, but I think there was more to it. Her name is Linda, Linda Kellar.'

Mrs Charles nodded. 'Yes, I remember Linda, and her mother.

I regret, however, that what passed between Linda and me must remain private.'

Cheryl avoided looking directly at the clairvoyant: she had a feeling that if she met her gaze, she would see straight through her. 'I think the real reason that Linda came to see you is because she's pregnant ... or worse. It has since occurred to me – and this is what is really worrying me – that she might've contracted a sexually transmitted disease and that she needed advice from someone outside the family as to what she should do about it.'

'If Linda had any concerns of that nature, she definitely did not confide them in me,' Mrs Charles assured her.

Cheryl continued to avoid Mrs Charles's gaze. She spoke petulantly. 'It was about me, wasn't it? That was why she came to see you. She hates me. So did her mother.'

Mrs Charles made no reply, and frightened by her lack of response, Cheryl gave her a quick, anxious look.

'No,' said Mrs Charles. 'I can assure you that Linda's concerns were for herself, and that it was in this sole area that I read the tarot for her as a means of guidance and help for the future.'

Cheryl sipped her tea: then, replacing her cup firmly in its saucer, and again, avoiding looking directly at Mrs Charles, she asked, 'Will you help me?'

'If this is the real reason why you contacted me, yes: but there must be no pretence between us. The slightest hint that you are not being completely truthful with me, and I regret that I will have to ask you to leave.'

There was a small silence. And then Cheryl asked, 'Do you know who I am?'

'I know only what you have thus far chosen to tell me.'

Cheryl drew in her breath and then, letting it out slowly, she said, 'I killed someone, a friend of mine....' She made a small gesture with one hand. 'It was years ago, when I was a teenager. I didn't mean to kill her, it wasn't premeditated murder. But I did kill her. We had a silly quarrel and I lost my temper. I pushed her and she fell into some water and drowned. It was as simple as that. I was questioned by the police, but I was never charged with her murder. My parents were given to understand that the investigation into my friend's death wasn't officially closed, but that there was insufficient evidence to mount a successful court case against me. The whole thing was more or less written off as an accidental death, although I know that the police and my friends, even members of my own family, have always believed that I killed my friend and that I shouldn't have got away with it.'

Mrs Charles didn't say anything for a moment or two. Then she asked, in a quiet voice, 'What is it that you seek from me?'

'I would like you to read the tarot for me and tell me if the decision I have made to confess to my having killed my friend is the right thing to do after all this time. I can't carry this burden of guilt any longer. My fiancé's mother and one of the detectives who investigated my friend's death, have, in one way or another, persecuted me and my family for years because of what I did. They are both gone now – dead, I mean – and that should've made all the difference, but it hasn't. If anything the guilt and the pressure I feel to confess are intensifying. I don't want to live with this hanging over me for the rest of my life. I am hopeful that after all this time, and bearing in mind how young and silly I was when I killed my friend, the case against me will be dropped. Getting married is a fresh start, and that's what I want it to be.'

Mrs Charles picked up the pack of tarot cards that she had placed earlier on the occasional table between them, and handed it to Cheryl. 'I want you to hold the cards lightly in both hands for me, please.'

Cheryl did as she had been instructed and then looked at Mrs Charles expectantly.

'Now, I want you to go through, very carefully and in your own time, the events that preceded your giving your friend a push which, you say, resulted in her death,' Mrs Charles went on.

Cheryl closed her eyes. 'I've been through this so many times,' she said wearily. 'I've admitted to you that I killed her. All I want is for you to tell me what will happen to me if I go to the police and confess. I'm so afraid—' She broke off suddenly.

'Afraid of what, Cheryl?' asked the clairvoyant quietly.

Cheryl made a choked little sound and then looked down at the pack of cards she was holding. It was a moment or two before she replied. 'I'm afraid that Barry will leave me if I go to the police and confess that I killed my friend.'

'Has he ever given you reason to suspect that he might turn his back on you if you made a confession of this nature to the police?'

Cheryl shook her head. 'No, he's always been very supportive of me in every way.'

'Then I see no reason for you to be afraid that the support he has always given you in the past will suddenly be withdrawn.'

'I've been in love with him for as long as I can remember,' Cheryl confided wistfully. 'Since we were four-year-olds and attended the same play school. That is what started it all that day between Valerie – my friend – and me. She was laughing at me for the way, she said, I chased after Barry all the time like a lovesick little puppy-dog. She said it was pathetic to watch and that Barry didn't know I was alive which, I have to admit, was probably true. Barry was always one for his mates in those days. And then she said something absolutely horrible and completely untrue. She said Barry had got her pregnant, and that his mother knew – she said she'd told his mother about the baby – and that Mrs Sowerby was backing her all the way.'

'Barry was present while this conversation between you and Valerie was taking place?'

Cheryl shook her head vigorously. 'No, of course not. Valerie and I were alone … well, not exactly alone. Six of us had gone to a place known as the gravel pit. This was after school one day. We often went there' – she shrugged – 'just to hang out. Valerie and me, and Barry and three of his mates. They, the boys, had gone off. One of them, Andrew, had some weed, and one of the others had brought along a couple of six packs of lager....'

Cheryl fell silent. Then she sighed. 'Anyway, after they'd drifted off, things turned really nasty between Valerie and me. I called her some dreadful names for the things she'd said about her and Barry, and I smacked her face, really hard. She just stood there and laughed at me and then she said she was going home. I was so angry with her that I followed her. I wanted to make her tell me the truth – that she'd made it all up about her and Barry and his mother. I think I knew deep down that it was all a lie: Valerie was always saying things about people that weren't true, just for the fun of it. She liked to see how they'd react and whether they'd do something about it. But I guess I was so angry and afraid that she might have been telling me the truth, that when we reached the actual gravel pit itself, I pushed her. Not really all that hard, but enough to make her lose her balance and fall down the side of it. She screamed ... I sometimes hear her screaming in my sleep' – she confessed, her natural scowl deepening – 'and then I turned and walked off. But while I was on my way back to find the boys who'd gone there with us that day, I suddenly got scared about what I'd done. That was when I went back to make sure she was all right. At least, I honestly believe this is what I *meant* to do, and I'm sure I did ... *I went back*.' She hesitated, tightening her grip on the tarot cards and fixing her gaze on her knuckles which had turned white. 'I swear I haven't imagined that this is what I did because it makes me feel better,' she insisted, a note of doubt nevertheless creeping into her voice, 'and Valerie was crawling up the side of the pit.'

'Then what happened?' asked Mrs Charles when Cheryl paused.

'Valerie started calling me names, so' – Cheryl shrugged faintly – 'I gave up and went back to look for the boys.' She looked at Mrs Charles almost fiercely. 'There's not a day that goes by that I don't think about what happened to her, you know, and some-times, it all gets muddled up in my head and I feel confused. I admit, though, that I lost my temper with her and that I deliber-ately pushed her into the gravel pit, but I thought she was OK. How was I to know that she was going to slide down the side of it for a second time and then drown?'

She fell silent, again shrugging faintly when Mrs Charles made no comment and merely looked at her expectantly, waiting for her to continue.

'I told them – the boys who were with us – that Valerie had gone off on her own and not to bother to wait for her. It was getting late and so we all started to walk home. We had to pass the gravel pit on our way and that was when we saw her. It was too late. She was already dead. The worst of it is that when one of the boys went down to her – it was Andrew, Andrew Tomlinson, who went down to see if she was all right – and he called up to us that he thought she was dead because he couldn't find a pulse, I was pleased.' Cheryl laughed drily. 'And what a price I am going to have to pay for that one moment of pure, unadulterated pleasure. You see, before I contacted you, I'd more or less made up my mind that I was going to confess to having killed Valerie, but now I've no choice: I'm being blackmailed.' She drew in her breath. 'By Andrew Tomlinson. He says he's got a story to tell, one he's sure Barry and the police would love to hear.'

Chapter forty-two

'WHAT HAPPENED NEXT?' ASKED MRS CHARLES.

'What happened next?' Cheryl echoed in a dry voice. 'My life was ruined, that's what happened next! My mother's health slowly deteriorated and over the last few weeks, since Jo Sowerby died, it has worsened.' She widened her eyes at the clairvoyant. 'I can't believe that something like this could happen: it's a living nightmare! Andrew Tomlinson has now stepped into Jo Sowerby's shoes and he is going to carry on where she left off. My family and I are never going to be free of Valerie Ward and left in peace.'

'I was actually referring to what happened to you and your friends in the days immediately following Valerie's death,' explained Mrs Charles.

Cheryl was silent for some moments. Then she said, 'Looking back now, I think that in any event, the friendships that had been there for a number of years, were coming to an end. We'd been slowly growing apart; wanting different things from life and ready to go our separate ways—'

Mrs Charles interrupted her. 'And yet at some point, you and Barry rekindled your friendship,' she pointed out.

Cheryl spoke wryly. 'That was Jo Sowerby's doing. She never meant things to turn out the way they have between Barry and me, and who knows, if it hadn't been for this obsession of hers to have me confess to killing Valerie, I very much doubt that Barry would've given me a second look. The last thing his mother would've wanted was to push us together, but when you think about it, this is exactly what she did when she never gave up trying to prove conclusively that I killed Valerie.'

With a heavy sigh, the young woman then went on, 'Anyway, to answer your question about what happened next.... Like I've said, we were drifting apart: we'd started picking on one another, finding fault all the time, and that day was no exception. Valerie's death was a kind of catalyst. We broke up immediately afterwards, perhaps out of embarrassment over what had happened – we couldn't face one another without remembering her and the last day we were all together – or that was it, we were simply ready to move on. It might even have been a mix of all three. I was going to say that Barry and I are the only ones left, certainly in this country. But now, Andrew Tomlinson is back. He and his family emigrated to New Zealand soon after Valerie died; I never thought we'd see him again. He told me he'd brought his grandmother back as she couldn't cope with the long flight on her own. She had apparently never really settled out there, and she wanted to come home. He's a journalist now, or so he said – has degrees in social studies and English literature; but I've no idea if any of this is true. Probably not. He's seen a means of making some easy money and he's about to grab it with both hands.'

'What of the other members of your little group, where are they now?' enquired Mrs Charles.

'One of the other boys committed suicide. We were all dreadfully upset when we heard he was dead – of us all, he was probably the nicest – and while nobody said anything directly to my face, I know it was generally accepted that what had happened to Valerie was behind his suicide. In other words, it was my fault, too, that he was dead. He was somebody else Valerie kept having nasty little digs at that day. He was an easy target, though: it didn't take much to upset him. It's one of the failings of being nice, isn't it? People take advantage of you. He was always the weakest link in the chain. He worshipped Valerie, and she enjoyed belittling him because of it. The fourth boy in our little clique was a real tearaway: I'm not excusing myself, but any mischief we got up to – we would dare one another to go shoplifting and then we'd parade our individual hauls to see who would come off best,' Cheryl confessed in a rueful voice, 'he would be the instigator and always outdid the rest of us. I was quite surprised when I found out that he'd gone off with his parents to do good works somewhere in Africa. My mother heard later that he'd contracted malaria and died. So there are now only three of us left – Barry, Andrew and me.'

'Have you made any arrangements with Andrew concerning this threat of his?'

Cheryl nodded. 'He's given me his mobile phone number and I'm to ring him after the weekend – as soon as Barry gets back from a conference he's attending – and tell him when he can come to our flat and see us.' She hesitated; looked at Mrs Charles thoughtfully. 'This is what is called a cold reading, isn't it? You get me to tell you everything you want to know about me and then you cleverly drip-feed it back to me. I'm supposed to go away feeling most impressed by what you've told me and marvelling at how much of what you've described from my past is accurate.' Cheryl gave her head a slow shake. 'I want answers; I don't need you to play clever guessing games with my life, telling me what I already know, thank you very much.'

'Cold readings do nothing more than enhance the status of the reader; they do precious little for the sitter who, as you've said, knows his or her past better than anybody. This is not what I am about, Cheryl. The questions I have asked you go beyond the standard cold reading you have described. The important thing to remember is this: the past is always there, walking in partnership with the present and the future and directly influencing them. I have encouraged you to speak of your past so that we can both move on from it. For my part, I will use this knowledge only to determine the present from it and what lies in your future. Your past, however, will now inevitably reveal itself clearly to me in the reading I will do for you; but as you've said, there is no need for me to tell you what you already know and at no time will I refer to it.'

Cheryl apologized. 'I'm sorry if I've been rude. I've become a shrew lately and I hate myself for it. I know of your reputation as a clairvoyant and I can't believe I've said those things to you. Please forgive me.' Her voice wavered a little. 'Help me.'

'Shuffle the cards for me, please, Cheryl,' said the clairvoyant simply.

Chapter forty-three

THE CLAIRVOYANT TOOK THE PACK OF CARDS FROM CHERYL. Acutely aware of the tension in the young woman, Edwina Charles began to deal out the first two cards in Cheryl's reading, at the same time quietly explaining the significance of the spread that she had chosen to use.

Glancing up at Cheryl, she said, 'The two cards I have placed before you – *The High Priestess* and the *Ten of Batons* or *Wands* – represent the influences of the past in relation to the present.'

Leaving a significant space after these two cards, which had been placed side by side, and continuing to place the cards in a horizontal line across the table, Mrs Charles dealt out three more cards. The first of these was *The Lovers* from the Major Arcana. The second of the three was *The Emperor*, again from the Major Arcana, and the third, the *Nine of Pentacles* from the Minor Arcana.

Mrs Charles looked up at Cheryl again. 'These three cards represent the present.'

Cheryl rolled her lips back and forth and nodded. Her hands were clasped together and she began to wring them slowly.

'There are two more cards in your reading,' Mrs Charles went on, 'and these will represent your future.'

Another significant space was left between the two cards she then placed down on the table and the preceding three cards. The first of the final two cards was *The Devil* from the Major Arcana, and the last was the *Eight of Swords* from the Minor Arcana.

No reference was made to the fact that all seven cards in Cheryl's reading were reversed, something that would not have been apparent to her as she was seated opposite the clairvoyant. The significance of a reversed card in a reading is in the alteration of its meaning and the influence it will have in relation to both a preceding card and that which will immediately follow it. In all instances, a reversed card, when dealt out either before or after an upright card, considerably weakens the meaning and influence of the latter card.

The clairvoyant was silent for some moments while she studied the cards. At length, she looked up at Cheryl and said, 'If, as you've said, Cheryl, you know of my reputation, then it is vital that you heed the warning I am about to give you and that you act upon it immediately and without question. Should you choose to ignore my warning, there is a strong possibility that another life will be lost: you will then have to bear the burden of guilt for this further death for the rest of your life, knowing that you had been warned of what might happen and that you chose to ignore what I am about to tell you. You have asked for my help, principally to advise you as to whether or not you should confess to the police that you killed your friend. My advice to you, based on my reading of the tarot cards you see before you, is that in no circumstances should you confess to having killed that young girl.'

Cheryl had paled. 'I don't understand: I killed her—'

Mrs Charles's voice cut firmly across hers. 'Furthermore, you must promise me that when you leave here, you will not let your fiancé's sister, Linda, out of your sight until he returns after the weekend. You must also promise me that you will speak to no one of the warning I have given you. Break your promise and you will have to face the consequences which, I cannot stress too strongly, will seriously compromise Linda's life.'

'This is ridiculous, I don't believe it!'

Mrs Charles said nothing.

'What on earth could Linda have to do with my confessing to having killed someone?' asked Cheryl incredulously.

'I cannot go into that with you as it would constitute a breach of confidentiality. You must simply trust me that what I have told you will almost certainly come to pass if you ignore my warning.'

Cheryl was shaking her head perplexedly. 'But Linda.... She

knows nothing of Valerie Ward. Barry told me his mother never discussed Valerie with her; and he hasn't, I'm sure of that. Linda is eight years younger than Barry and me. She was only six when Valerie died.'

'Her age then and now is irrelevant, as is the fact that what happened to Valerie has never been discussed with her. Linda has been inexorably drawn into the circumstances surrounding her death, and because of this, I want you to give me your word that you will bring her back to me tomorrow afternoon at three o'clock.'

'Why, what for?'

'It is now absolutely essential that I finish the reading I did for her when she came to see me.'

Cheryl was frowning. She spoke impatiently. 'I simply cannot see how she could be involved in my worries and concerns.'

Mrs Charles regarded her in silence for a moment or two. Then she said, 'It will doubtless come as a shock to you to learn that my reading of the tarot for Linda was not intended for her. She, quite innocently and understandably in the circumstances, misappropriated a gift of a tarot reading that her mother, had she lived, would have asked you to accept prior to your marrying her son. The two tarot readings I have given – Linda's and yours – are what bind you and Linda together, and in so doing, have revealed the threat to her life.'

'Jo was giving me a tarot reading as a wedding gift? What did she expect?' Cheryl's eyebrows went up. There was a sharp edge to her voice. 'That you would see my guilt in the tarot and force me to confess? What a hoot that is! I came to you of my own free will and have confessed, anyway. My God, what Jo wouldn't give to be a fly on the wall and hear me say that!'

'You must put any antipathy that you feel for her behind you and trust me, Cheryl. Simply do as I ask and you will greatly lessen the risk to Linda's life.'

'I–' Cheryl broke off abruptly. Then, with a faint shrug, she said, 'I don't understand any of this, but all right then, I'll do as you ask. I'll bring her to you tomorrow afternoon.' She hesitated; looked at the clairvoyant searchingly. 'But what if she won't listen to me? She can be very stubborn.'

Mrs Charles gazed past her. It was a moment or two before she responded. Then, looking directly back at Cheryl, she said, in a quiet voice, 'She'll listen to you, Cheryl. Linda knows her life is in danger.'

Chapter forty-four

EDWINA CHARLES AND DAVID SAYER WALKED SLOWLY INTO THE village. It was the following morning and Mrs Charles was on her way to catch the 10 a.m. bus into Gidding to see Joyce Cooper, David was on an errand for his aunt.

They had been discussing means of coping with Miss Sayer's increasing irascibility with everyone and everything, which David had described as being hell to live with, when, abruptly, he changed the subject.

'So ... nothing new to report.'

Aware of a slight mocking tone in his voice, and that he had actually made a statement and was not asking a question, Mrs Charles looked at him thoughtfully.

'Jo Sowerby – that's your current pet cause, isn't it?' He grinned.

Mrs Charles smiled faintly, but made no response.

'Sorry,' he said. 'But you really are on a hiding to nothing with this one.'

'Perhaps. Right now, I'm rather more concerned with her daughter's well-being. There have been some surprising developments, Superintendent.'

'Pardon?' He halted abruptly, leaving her to walk on alone for a short distance before likewise coming to a complete standstill. She looked back at him and waited for him to catch up to her.

Mrs Charles did not repeat herself. 'And when I'm sure what they mean,' she went on coolly, 'I can promise that you will be the first to know.'

They walked on. David wasn't sure what to say. He knew what

he thought, though. Mrs Charles was losing it: she had let her past successes go to her head. It surprised him a little, as he had always held her in high regard and couldn't recall ever having seriously questioned her judgement, even if at times, as a former high-ranking police officer, her methods of deduction were often quite incomprehensible to him.

Time, David, to step back and let her get on with it, he said to himself a few minutes later as he watched her board the bus for Gidding. *No sense in two of us making fools of ourselves!*

Chapter forty-five

JOYCE COOPER WAS WATERING THE PLANTS IN HER CONSERVATORY when Edwina Charles rang her doorbell a little over an hour later. It was a large conservatory, recently built but on stylishly attractive Victorian lines, and it was here that Joyce invited Mrs Charles to sit with her, on comfortable, plumply upholstered cane furniture which faced out over her neat, well-stocked garden, while they discussed what Joyce had to tell her.

'I've had to think long and hard about this,' confessed Joyce with a small grimace, 'largely because most of it is gossip – rumours that went round town at the time and which I want you to understand I cannot therefore guarantee are entirely true. It's just that it seemed so important to you to get to the bottom of those unpleasant dreams that young girl was experiencing – the mock funeral and all that went with it....' Joyce's voice tailed off apologetically. She widened her eyes expressively at Mrs Charles. 'I really wouldn't want this to go any further than the two of us. As a former shopkeeper, I've seen the harm gossip can do to people.'

Mrs Charles nodded. 'I understand.'

Joyce was silent for a moment. Then she said, 'After you left the other day, I couldn't help thinking that I'd seen the young man before – the one who paid for the flowers that I later delivered to the Baxters' home. My memory is terrible these days – I think I might have mentioned that – but it finally came to me where it was that I'd seen him. Believe it or not, it was actually in my shop. He was employed by Kempthornes, the funeral directors – not on a regular basis, you understand, but getting work experience during the summer holidays while he was waiting to start college.

I know it seems a strange thing for a young person to want to do ... work in a funeral parlour – he couldn't have been any more than eighteen or nineteen at the time – but he apparently considered it was going to be useful to him later on in his chosen career, whatever that was ... writing horror stories, for all I know,' she put in with a wry grin. 'To the best of my knowledge, he never took up full employment with Kempthornes after he'd finished his studies, and I never saw him again after that summer, either in my shop or elsewhere around town.'

Mrs Charles looked at her enquiringly. 'And the gossip?'

'Ah, yes, the gossip.' Joyce sighed. 'It started with one of my customers who ran a restaurant and ordered flowers from me on a fairly regular basis. We got to know each other quite well over the years and when her husband died – which was sometime during that summer – Kempthornes handled the funeral arrangements. She called in there unexpectedly one day to discuss his funeral with Mrs Kempthorne and she overheard her addressing the young man in question in particularly endearing terms. They were in the chapel of rest and hadn't heard her come in. My customer said that it was most embarrassing for them all – particularly for Mrs Kempthorne. She tried to brush the incident off as a joke, but my customer told me that it was pretty obvious what was going on between the two of them. Then I later heard from another customer, who had sons around the same age as Mrs Kempthorne's, and who were friendly with her boys, that the young man and Mrs Kempthorne were having a steamy affair and that her sons objected to it strongly. Evidently, it was the talk of the town, although I hadn't previously heard anything of this side of the young man's involvement with her. Anyway, he apparently went off to college a short while later and that was the end of it. Or so I imagine. I later heard from a number of independent sources that Mrs Kempthorne had something of a reputation for liking the company of men many years her junior.'

'This gossip ... did you hear it before or after the incident at the Baxters?' asked Mrs Charles.

'Well, I'd seen him before that happened, probably three or four times, and the gossip came later.'

'Do you know his name?'

Joyce shook her head regretfully. 'If I knew it, it's lost for all time, although frankly, I doubt that I ever did know it. I just thought I'd tell you about this young man's involvement with Mrs Kempthorne in case you wanted to try and find out from her who he was and if she can help you with the name of the person who actually sent him to me in connection with the hoax flower order for the Baxters.' She hesitated. 'It's crossed my mind that Mrs Kempthorne might've been behind it all, but that doesn't make sense, does it? I was going to say, a respectable woman like her....' She grinned sheepishly. 'But I think you know what I mean. I hardly think someone in her profession would allow herself to become involved in a cruel prank like that, do you? I mean, why? Surely, if the truth ever got out, it would do terrible harm to her business.'

Chapter forty-six

SEAN KEMPTHORNE LOOKED UP AS THE STREET DOOR OPENED AND Edwina Charles walked in. He was standing at the desk in Reception and had been gazing intently at the computer monitor in front of him. He was considering closing up for the day, smiling to himself at the unintentional pun he had made when he thought of local business in Gidding after midday on a Saturday as being dead.

He didn't greet Mrs Charles, merely smirked at her and said, 'I thought we'd be seeing you again.' Then, turning his head on one side and directing his voice in the general direction of the Chapel of Rest, he called out, 'Mother, your worst nightmare has just materialized before my very eyes.'

It was a moment or two before Mrs Kempthorne appeared, the look she gave Mrs Charles only fractionally less hostile than the tone of voice she used in greeting her. She did not wait for any response from her visitor. She went straight on, 'I thought I'd made it quite clear the last time you called that I was unable to be of any assistance to you.'

'This shouldn't take long, Mrs Kempthorne,' said Mrs Charles. 'I'll get straight to the point. I would like you to give me the name of the young man who was employed here during the time that one of your cars was misappropriated and later found at the home of the Baxter family.'

Mrs Kempthorne gave a false laugh. 'Good heavens, you can't expect me to remember his name after all this time! That was years ago and he was only with us for a matter of a few weeks before leaving Gidding, as I understood it, to attend university –

and before you ask, there will be no records of his employment
with us as there never were any, we had a private arrangement.
Without going into morbid details, he was seeking work experience specifically in our line of business and we were happy to
comply with his request, which was only ever intended to be
short-term. Now, if you'll excuse me, I happen to be rather busy
at the moment. Please do not trouble me again. Should you do so,
I will have no alternative but to take the matter further with the
police. I hope I have made myself clear. I will not be harassed in
this fashion by anyone.'

Mrs Charles looked at her thoughtfully and then she nodded
her head and turned to leave. At the door, she paused and looked
back at Mrs Kempthorne and her son, who hadn't moved from
the desk. If the look on his face were anything to go by, he had
found the conversation between the two women vastly amusing.

'I will not call again,' Mrs Charles promised Mrs Kempthorne.
'I returned here today as a matter of courtesy to you and in the
hope that you would give me the information I want without *my*
taking the matter further and perhaps, in the process, raking up
old issues that you, personally, would prefer were left undisturbed
and forgotten. Please be assured, however, that this is not the end
of my interest in that young man. I will continue to ask questions
elsewhere until I get the answers I want about him regarding his
term of employment with you.'

Mrs Kempthorne and her son exchanged looks. He grinned
and raised his shoulders a fraction. Mrs Kempthorne looked back
at Mrs Charles and then, without a word, she glanced at her son
and indicated to the small notepad on the desk. He picked up a
ballpoint pen and then looked at his mother and waited, a faint
smirk playing at the corners of his mouth. His mother nodded her
head at him, just the once, and he wrote something down quickly
on the notepad, then briskly tore off the slip of paper and,
brushing past her, went up to Mrs Charles and handed it to her.

Mrs Charles glanced at the name that he had written down and
then, looking up at Mrs Kempthorne, she nodded and said,
simply, 'Good-day.'

Edwina Charles sat in a window seat, gazing intently at the activity on the other side of the motorway and seeing none of it. Every so often since boarding the bus for the return journey to Little Gidding, she would glance at the name she had been given by Sean Kempthorne, each time telling herself the same thing. If she accepted as being correct, Linda's subconscious fear that her mother had instigated the theft of the Kempthornes' funeral car, and that she had also arranged for the flowers to be delivered to the Baxters' home, it made perfect sense that this particular young man had been used for both purposes, and that he had done her bidding without question.

So why wasn't she happy about it?

Chapter forty-seven

THREE O'CLOCK CAME AND WENT WITH NO SIGN OF LINDA. AT A quarter past three, Cheryl, using her mobile phone, assured Edwina Charles that she and Linda were on their way: there had been a major accident on the motorway which had reduced traffic to a single line in a five-mile tailback that was moving at a snail's pace.

It was almost four o'clock when finally, Linda jumped out of Cheryl's car and hurried up the path to where Mrs Charles waited on her front doorstep. Linda's body language, her mumbled apologies for her lateness and a refusal to look Mrs Charles directly in the eye, clearly indicated that so far as she was concerned, the sooner she put this visit behind her, the better.

As Linda sat waiting to hear why Mrs Charles had wanted to see her again, she was nervous and fidgety. She had successfully held out for most of the morning in resisting Cheryl's insistence that this further visit to the clairvoyant was in her best interests. Linda had been deeply suspicious of Cheryl's motives and had been adamant that if there were things that needed to be talked over, Barry was the person to do this with, they were no business of anyone else. It had only been the thought of having to put up with Cheryl's going on at her about it all weekend that had made Linda relent. Cheryl had refused to give a coherent reason for insisting on her moving in with her for the weekend, choosing instead to insinuate that this was something that Barry and she had discussed between themselves before he had left. She had stressed that Barry expected Linda to comply, which, if this were true, had also awakened a niggling fear in Linda of what might happen during the long wait ahead of her before he returned and she could confide in him. The minutes and hours had never seemed so long: the slightest noise, footsteps walking past along the road outside the flat, a breeze murmuring softly in the leaves of an old chestnut tree on the opposite side of the road, had never seemed so threatening.

Mrs Charles did not waste any time with preliminary small talk. 'This, Linda, is why I wanted to see you again.' As she spoke, slowly and deliberately, she dealt out the cards from Linda's reading on to the occasional table between them.

Linda avoided looking at them. 'I haven't forgotten what you told me the other day,' she said defensively. 'I was going to discuss with my brother what I should do about going to college when he gets back on Monday.'

Mrs Charles made no immediate response. It was as if Linda hadn't spoken. The clairvoyant's gaze remained fixed firmly on the cards. 'I think, Linda,' she said at length, 'that since you left here the other day, you have discovered for yourself what was in your tarot reading. This card' – she pointed to the *Queen of Swords* and then looked up at Linda – 'represents your mother and the strong influence she had, and in some respects, is still having over every aspect of your life. The card before it, the *Five of Deniers*, tells me clearly that you have made a very serious error of judgement relating to your mother and as a result of this, you have placed your life in very grave danger. You are concealing something concerning your mother's death, Linda – I have no doubt for what you consider to be the best of reasons – to protect yourself and your brother and his fiancée, but unfortunately, in so doing, you have set in motion a series of events that, should you persist in suppressing the knowledge the tarot and I know you have relating to your mother, all you will achieve is the very thing you most fear. It may even be too late for you to reverse the tide that has been sweeping you along ever since we last spoke. Only you can change things, Linda. Your life, quite literally, is in your own hands. Don't throw it away.'

Linda kept her gaze lowered: she picked nervously at the cloth in her jeans. 'I'll talk to Barry; he'll know what to do.'

'You must face this alone, Linda. It is time for you to take responsibility for your actions, and the longer you delay in accepting this inevitability, the greater the risk to your life.'

Linda did not look up. She splayed out her hands on her thighs and appeared to be studying her fingernails.

'The attack on your mother in the cemetery, while not the direct cause of her death, resulted in her fatal heart attack. The fact remains that the intent of the attack on her was to kill her.' The clairvoyant had spoken firmly, but now she softened her voice. 'If you don't know this for sure, then it's something you have reason to feel might be true. Face that fear, Linda, and the threat to your life will greatly diminish.'

'But it won't go away altogether, will it?' Linda spoke in a faintly hostile mumble. She twitched her shoulders irritably.

Mrs Charles said nothing.

There was a long silence and then Linda said, in a small, barely audible voice, 'I know who killed my mother.'

Linda looked up at Mrs Charles when there was no response from her. 'I know her murderer as Eddie Nuttall, but that isn't his real name. It's Andrew, not Eddie, and he arranged to meet my mother. He sent her a photograph of himself so that she would recognize him when they met. I found it in one of her jackets. I don't know who he really is, or what exactly it is that he wanted with my mother, I just know that they met and....' She fell silent.

'How do you know they met, Linda?'

'Because—' Linda hesitated. 'The police got it wrong. My mother wasn't attacked anywhere near my father's grave. She never went near it: she hated him. If my mother and this Eddie or Andrew, whoever, met in the cemetery – and I'm positive they did meet there on the night she died – it was at the graveside of one of her friends and her friend's daughter, Valerie. They were buried together, in the same plot, and my mother went there every day, or rather, it was mostly at night, to speak to them.'

She looked up at Mrs Charles with a faint scowl. 'I know that sounds crazy, but this is what she did, without fail. I'd go out looking for her some nights when she hadn't come home, and I'd find her talking to them, promising that she'd make things right so that they could rest in peace. She worked nights in a pub on the other side of the cemetery, which was why it was usually at night that she was in there. That grave is on the opposite side of the cemetery to my father's. I don't know why the police said she was attacked near his grave because it never would have happened, *never*!'

Linda paused; was abruptly lost in thought, miles away. The expression in her eyes was difficult to read, but she appeared to be working something out in her head – either that or something had suddenly occurred to her which she needed to think through. There was a subtle change in her manner which Mrs Charles found disturbing. Moments before, the events of that night had been convincingly set before her, and then something – something Linda had just said, perhaps – had made the girl stop and reconsider. Or maybe it was simply that she had finally found the courage to speak out that had made her want to pause and go back over everything she had said. It crossed Mrs Charles's mind that there was a possibility that Linda was not being completely honest with her in an effort to throw her off the scent. *But the scent of what?* Mrs Charles asked herself. And was this particular girl clever enough for something like that? Mrs Charles doubted it. But the thought persisted: something was wrong.

Just as abruptly, Linda was back in the moment. 'I should know,' she went on irritably. 'I was the one who had to go looking for her when she didn't come home after work, wasn't I? It was always left to me: I was the one who couldn't sleep at night because I thought she might be lying somewhere in a gutter. Nothing would have made my mother walk anywhere near my father's grave. I don't care if the police say they found evidence that told them it was there that she was attacked. Somebody deliberately put it there for them to find and think that. This is how I know she was murdered.... The person who attacked her, meant to kill her.'

'Why would her killer do something like that, Linda – plant false evidence at your father's grave?' asked the clairvoyant softly.

'Because—' Linda fell silent and thought for a moment or two. 'Because they, he, Eddie – Andrew,' she corrected herself irritably, 'didn't want anyone to know where she actually was when he killed her. And that–' She broke off.

'Finish what you were going to say, Linda.'

'That means he met her because of Valerie Ward, something to do with what happened to her and Cheryl.' She looked at Mrs Charles earnestly and her eyes filled with tears. 'I couldn't tell the police: I couldn't have it start all over again about Valerie. Barry and I had lived with it, my mother's obsession with her and her hatred of Cheryl, my brother's fiancée, for years. I just wanted it to end.'

'But it hasn't ended, has it?'

'No.' Linda shook her head. 'It's just got worse. First my mother and then Roy Adams, the man I blame for worsening my mother's drink problem by feeding her obsession with that dead girl. He, Andrew – the man in the photograph – killed him, too. He shot him in cold blood. It was in all the papers.'

'How do you know this, Linda?'

'I was there, at Roy's home, when it happened. Roy took me there after I left here the other day. He followed me here and was waiting for me when I came out.'

Mrs Charles looked at her thoughtfully. 'You actually saw this Andrew shoot him?'

Linda shook her head. 'No, I only heard the shot that killed him. By the time I got to Roy, he was dead and no one else was there.'

'So you don't really know for sure who shot him?'

'Yes, I do.' The scowl was back on Linda's face. 'Andrew deliberately hid the clothes he was wearing when he shot Roy, in my mother's washing machine to incriminate me. They were covered in blood. I got rid of them as soon as I found them. I put them in a bin bag and then threw them off a bridge that's not far from where I live, into the river. I was afraid the police would discover that I was there at Roy's place when he was shot and that I'd be blamed for having killed him. Or at least, for having been some sort of accessory. I am so afraid. Eddie – I mean, Andrew, is going to kill Barry and Cheryl. I don't know why, I just know this is what is going to happen and that it's all somehow tied up with

Valerie Ward. That stupid dream I keep having about a funeral car … it's not coming just for me, it's coming for them, too – Barry and Cheryl.'

Linda brushed away her tears with the back of one of her hands. 'I just hoped that if I kept quiet about everything, it would all go away … I mean, now that my mother is dead. I didn't know that Roy would be killed. If I'd spoken out, he would still be alive, wouldn't he?'

It was a moment or two before Mrs Charles responded. She had lowered her eyes to the cards again, although there was nothing there that she didn't already know. 'No, Linda,' she replied at length. 'The die was cast for all of you – for your mother, Roy Adams, Cheryl, and you and your brother – when your mother either arranged, or agreed to meet, the man in the photograph you found.'

'I'm right, aren't I?' said the girl in a shocked voice. 'He's going to kill me, all of us, one by one. *But why me?* I haven't done anything wrong.'

'I'm afraid you have, Linda. You turned your back on your one definite chance of salvation by not going to the police immediately with what you know of the attack on your mother, and now it is too late.'

Linda looked frightened. 'I don't understand. I haven't talked to anyone about any of this – only you, just now.'

'And you mustn't. If I cannot persuade you to go to the police with this information right away, then you must at least promise me that you will not tell anyone else.'

Linda was shaking her head. 'The police won't believe me. It all fits together much better their way. They're going to think I'm becoming obsessed and that I've gone loopy, like my mother and Roy Adams. They'll probably even insist on breathalysing me to see if I've been drinking,' she finished on a bitter note.

Mrs Charles looked at her for a very long moment. She was right; the police would listen to what she had to say, but that was a long way short of believing her claim that Jo Sowerby never went near her husband's grave. The evidence they had discovered at the alleged scene of her attack was overwhelmingly in favour of it having been there, at his graveside, that it had taken place.

The room grew dark and cold, as if a giant shadow had passed across the sun, momentarily blocking out its rays and warmth.

The clairvoyant knew what it meant. She had done what she could, everything but save Linda from herself.

Chapter forty-eight

'IF IT'S NOT A RUDE QUESTION, WHAT WAS THAT ALL ABOUT?' ASKED David Sayer when he called on Edwina Charles shortly before five o'clock that evening to collect the dozen free-range eggs her brother had bought at a neighbouring farm on behalf of David's aunt and then left with Mrs Charles.

She looked puzzled.

'The young woman who came hurtling out of here ten minutes ago.' David looked thoroughly bemused. 'She jumped into the car that was standing out the front and then by the time I got close enough to see what was going on, she and the female driver were having a right old ding-dong. The driver was gripping the steering wheel so tightly I thought she was going to rip it out and crown the other girl with it. Then she gunned the engine and they took off. The last look I got of the pair of them, the one in the passenger-seat was in floods of tears.'

'The girl you saw leaving here was Linda Kellar and the driver of the car was Cheryl Baxter,' said Mrs Charles.

'Happy families, eh?'

'It's worse than that, I'm afraid.'

'Not more grist for the Sowerby mill?' He gave her a sour look.

'I really think it's time Mr Merton and I had a little talk,' said Mrs Charles.

David shook his head. 'If it's got anything to do with Jo Sowerby, forget it. He's had Jo Sowerby and anything and everything to do with her up to here.' He chucked himself under the chin.

Mrs Charles was silent.

'Look, I can see you're worried,' he went on, 'and I appreciate that you must feel some distress over what happened to Jo Sowerby after she'd been to see you, but you can't hold yourself responsible for her death and keep on like this, trying to make amends for what I think you see as your failure to help her.'

'No one could help Jo Sowerby, least of all me, Superintendent,' said Mrs Charles with a small, dismissive gesture. 'From what I've learnt of her obsession with Valerie Ward's death, she'd been on a collision course over it for years. It amazes me that it has taken this long finally for everything to come to a head. I say finally, but we are not quite there yet. Linda Kellar is now caught up in her mother's obsession, and if she doesn't heed the advice I gave her this afternoon, which is to go to the police with what she believes to be a mistake they have made over her mother's death—'

He cut her off. 'Dear God, Madame, whatever you do don't let Merton know you think there's a possibility that a mistake has been made over her death!'

Mrs Charles made no comment, merely handed David the slip of paper that Sean Kempthorne had given her. 'There is something I would like you to do for me, please, and if you do this one thing, I promise that thereafter, I will never again mention Jo Sowerby's name or anything to do with her family and Valerie Ward. I can't really explain why I should be bothered by the name you see there, but I am. I dare say this will place you in an awkward position with Mr Merton, but it would go a long way towards putting my mind at rest if he would be kind enough to let me know everything he can about that young man. Hopefully, there will be nothing for him to tell me.'

David gave her an odd look.

She lifted her shoulders a little in a resigned gesture. 'Yes, I know I'm letting this get to me, but,' she sighed, 'I'll be happier once I know that I can close this particular door. I can only stress that it is really very important to me to have this information.'

He looked away from her, scratching his head. His expression had hardened. He was not happy. 'OK. That's the card I'll play, then, when approaching Merton, and we can only hope he's in a charitable mood and that he'll play ball.' David frowned at her.

'You must promise me, though, that if he agrees and I get this information for you, you'll let go.'

'If I can, Superintendent, only if I can.'

Mrs Charles was surprised to find an envelope fixed securely in the letter-slot in her front door when she returned from her brother's home later that evening. While she was out, David had called again with the information she had wanted and had hastily scrawled a note to her on the envelope itself. She read it thoughtfully.

Madame – I put up my hands and confess that I chickened out and called in a favour I was owed by an old mate who has promised to keep shtum so far as you know who is concerned. No dramatic result, I'm afraid. With the exception of one fairly minor motoring misdemeanour, the focus of your attention would appear to be a model citizen! Cheers, David.

Mrs Charles opened the envelope and took out the slip of paper that was inside it. To the name that was already on it, David had added the details of the motoring offence, the miscreant's occupation, his home address and the amount he had been fined.

She returned the slip of paper to the envelope with a thoughtful frown and then reread David's message. 'The definition of a dramatic result, though, very much depends on what one is looking for, doesn't it, Superintendent?' she murmured.

Chapter forty-nine

EDWINA CHARLES STOOD FOR A MOMENT CONTEMPLATING HER brother's brand new motor car before reluctantly climbing in alongside him. Cyril, a hitherto fanatical motor cyclist, had recently acquired the car in acknowledgment, he claimed, of his advancing years. As he was only in his early forties, Mrs Charles was more inclined to think that his desire to dispose of two wheels in favour of four was more likely to be in deference to the high winds and squally weather conditions of the previous winter. Exactly how Cyril had managed to pass the necessary driving tests for both vehicles would, for Mrs Charles, forever remain one of life's greater mysteries. There was always the possibility, of course, that he had struck examiners of a like-minded persuasion who shared both his interest in UFOs and his hopes for physical contact with the ETs which Cyril sincerely believed covertly monitored earth's inhabitants' every move!

No one could accuse Cyril of driving fast. He kept strictly to all speed limits, as required by law. He had a problem with traffic lights, though: he simply didn't see them, or if he did, thought they were intended for everybody but himself. A leisurely Sunday morning drive with Cyril was, therefore, neither an experience to anticipate with any degree of enthusiasm or excitement, nor to be endured with one's eyes wide open. But Mrs Charles had been faced with no alternative.

Since early morning, a strong sense of foreboding had steadily increased to the point where she simply had to override her reluctance to approach her brother with an urgent request for transport. There was no public bus service from the village into

Gidding on Sundays, no nearby rail service, and a distance of twenty-five miles made for a long walk on a hot Sunday morning. There was nothing more she could do to save Linda Kellar from herself – truth be told, it had always been too late; Linda would never want to accept or even see that she was the mistress of her own fate and act accordingly.

Having finally read the tarot for Cheryl Baxter, and regardless of Jo Sowerby's undeniably spurious motive in making this reading a gift to her future daughter-in-law, Mrs Charles considered herself to be under an obligation to do what she could to help the young woman now that she was allegedly facing a threat of blackmail. Jo Sowerby had wanted the truth, and, in part, she had got it. Cheryl had finally surrendered: she had held out against Jo for as long as she could and had Jo not died, would now have willingly admitted to whatever she had demanded of her. But that didn't mean she had to surrender likewise to blackmail, or that anyone had the right to carry on from where Jo had left off and in all probability, persecute her indefinitely.

The last thing Mrs Charles had asked Linda before the young woman had left late the previous afternoon, was if she might know where Eddie (or should that be Andrew?) could be located. Linda had reluctantly given her his address in town. He presented a confused picture. On the one hand, if the accusation Linda had levelled at him, were correct, he was guilty of having murdered her mother and Roy Adams; on the other hand, if Cheryl's accusation were correct, he was a potential blackmailer, this latter accusation pointing to his knowing a good deal more about what went on at the gravel pit on the day that Valerie Ward had died than anyone would have previously supposed. Was this a discovery that Jo Sowerby had made when, as Linda believed had happened, Andrew Tomlinson and Jo had met in the cemetery, and was whatever he knew about that day what had cost Jo her life? There was a possibility that his alleged plan to blackmail Cheryl had initially been at Jo's suggestion in the hope that this would put further pressure on the young woman to confess: it would certainly fit in with Jo's obsessively muddled thinking. But this didn't tie in with everything else that Mrs Charles had learnt about him. Did Jo Sowerby send for him, or had he returned to England of his own accord with his unsettled grandmother in tow, but with a secret agenda of murder and blackmail in mind?

During the drive into Gidding, Mrs Charles tried to analyse her feelings about the young man. He should be the vital missing piece in what was proving to be an increasingly bizarre jigsaw puzzle, but despite everything that she had been told about him by both Linda and Cheryl, and for reasons she couldn't explain to herself, she could only see him as part of the puzzle and belonging, if anywhere, on its periphery. She frowned thoughtfully to herself. What that would mean, then, was that she had all the pieces and for some reason, she simply couldn't see where to place them in their correct positions to make the whole picture....

Mrs Charles suddenly realized that they were approaching the outskirts of town.

'Once we reach Gidding, Cyril,' she said quickly, a trace of anxiety in her voice, 'I'll warn you well in advance when I see traffic lights up ahead of us.'

'I can see them for myself,' he said, glaring at her.

'Yes, I know you can see them, Cyril. That's not the point, is it?'

Chapter Fifty

CYRIL HAD SHARED DAVID SAYER'S OPPOSITION TO HIS SISTER'S determination to delve deeper into what she believed to be the background to Jo Sowerby's death, and had likewise advised her to let go when she had told him of her intention to seek out Linda's mysterious Eddie who was, without a doubt, Andrew Tomlinson, the fifth member and, according to Cheryl Baxter, would-be blackmailer of the infamous gravel pit six.

'You take care,' Cyril advised his sister with a scowl as she indicated to him to pull up outside a house where a young man was repointing the front brick wall. 'I'll be watching.'

'Thank you, Cyril,' said Mrs Charles with a solemn smile, getting out of the car.

The young man paused at his work and looked round questioningly as Mrs Charles stepped up to him and spoke his name.

'Yes,' he replied, eyeing her suspiciously. 'I'm Andrew Tomlinson: who's asking?'

Mrs Charles introduced herself, adding, 'I'm Cheryl Baxter's clairvoyant. I was retained by Mrs Josephine Sowerby whom, I believe, you knew—'

'So?' He cut in abruptly. The expression in his eyes had become guarded. 'This is supposed to mean something to me, is it?'

'If, as Cheryl has led me to believe, you propose to blackmail her about her involvement in the death of Valerie Ward some years ago, yes, I'm quite sure it should mean something to you.'

'That silly cow has really got her knickers in a twist, if that's what she's told you.'

'You deny threatening her in this fashion?'

He smirked a little. 'The only thing I'll admit to, and quite frankly, I don't see why I should, or that it's any of your business, was a brief moment of pleasure in watching her reaction to seeing me again after all these years. I won't pretend, I don't like Cheryl, I never did. She always was a hanger-on. What Barry Kellar sees in that waste of space, I'll never know. He was far too ambitious to tie himself down with someone like her.'

He paused and ran a speculative eye over Mrs Charles. 'Even as a kid, I thought Jo Sowerby was flaky, but this beats all. She actually hired – or should that be, *sicked*? – a clairvoyant on to Cheryl?' He laughed drily. 'No prizes for guessing why! You were supposed to bring Cheryl to her knees and make her finally confess to murdering Valerie, weren't you?'

'That's very perceptive of you,' Mrs Charles responded coolly. 'In which case, you will probably have no qualms about telling me why, following your return here from New Zealand, you agreed to meet Mrs Sowerby in the Gidding cemetery.'

'Excuse me?' His expression hardened. 'I never met Jo anywhere, least of all in a cemetery.'

'That's not what Linda Kellar seems to think.'

'That little airhead?' He smiled coldly. 'Don't tell me she's finally figured out who I am?'

'She found the photograph you sent her mother so that she would recognize you when you met.'

Andrew Tomlinson, for the first time, seemed mildly concerned. 'Now wait a minute.... All right, I was supposed to meet Jo – and I hasten to add, this wasn't my idea, it was my mother's: we were sick to death of Jo going on about Cheryl. Hardly a month would go by without another letter from her, and it has really worn my mother down. She's not in the best of health and Jo had become a real pest. I meant to meet her to try and get her to leave off, but I guess you could say I was overtaken by events; she had a heart attack and died.'

'But you don't deny that you stalked her daughter, calling your-self Eddie.'

'I met Linda purely by chance at a local club one night, and in the circumstances, once I knew who she was, I thought it best not to use my real name. I didn't know how much she knew about Valerie and the rest of it and, as I didn't expect our relationship to last beyond a few nights out together, I didn't see the harm in using another name. Why complicate matters?'

'But you did complicate matters, didn't you? When you left bloodstained clothing in her family's washing machine—'

Mrs Charles broke off. Andrew had opened his mouth, as if to say something. He put a hand to the plain gold ear-ring he was wearing in his left earlobe and then tugged on it gently. Mrs Charles waited for him to deny the accusation, but he remained silent. She could see that he was thinking something through, and then after a moment, he said, 'So that was what was in the black bin bag. I followed Linda and saw her throw it off a bridge. I thought she was up to something, but when I got to the bridge and looked to see what had happened to the bag, it had disappeared – been caught up in the river and carried off on the current, I guess.' He grinned crookedly. 'Who am I supposed to have killed?'

'She believes you shot Roy Adams, one of the detectives—'

'I know who Roy Adams is, was,' he cut in curtly.

'Linda was at his home the day he was shot.'

His eyes opened wide. 'My God, she's even crazier than her mother was if she says she saw me there, because believe me, Mrs Clairvoyant, I have never been anywhere near Roy Adams or his home. Not now, not ever! One crazy was enough to deal with, thank you. If you're looking for pointers as to who really killed him, I'd start looking a lot closer to home – if you get my meaning and follow my drift,' he sneered. 'With Jo out of the way, that only left Roy to get rid of and then you could consider yourself home and hosed, couldn't you?'

'You surely don't think Cheryl killed Roy?'

'Why not?'

'Because it wasn't in the tarot reading I did for her,' said Mrs Charles simply.

He burst out laughing. Breaking off, he said, 'Sorry, but you don't really expect me to believe that you could see something like that in a pack of kiddies' playtime cards, do you?'

Mrs Charles made no response. 'There's just one thing I'm really curious about,' she confessed after a moment. 'I know you said that Jo Sowerby had become a pest with her letter writing, but I find it hard to accept that your mother pressured you into seeing what you could do to dissuade Jo from continuing to contact you about bringing Cheryl to justice. I think this was a decision you made personally, otherwise why not drop the matter once you learnt that Jo was dead?'

'I don't follow you.'

'Oh, I think you do, Andrew. Why would you arrange to meet Cheryl when her fiancé returns tomorrow evening when, finally, you could put Valerie's death behind you once and for all?'

He eyed her thoughtfully. 'You're determined to make something of this, aren't you?'

'So I've been told,' she said in a cold voice. 'And I will make something of it, Andrew: I can promise you that.'

He shook his head slowly. Then, with a sigh, he said, 'You talk about putting Valerie's death behind me. It's not possible, it never will be.' He paused, looking up at the clear blue sky and squinting a little. 'You see, I killed her.'

Mrs Charles looked him, puzzled. 'I don't understand....'

He placed the trowel he had been using, on the wall, gazed at it for a moment, and then he said, 'I think you'd better come inside.'

Chapter Fifty-one

A FLASH OF BRIGHT, LATE AFTERNOON SUNLIGHT CAUGHT EDWINA Charles's eyes, momentarily blinding her as she said goodbye to her brother at her front gate over two hours later and then turned away to go inside. It came from the direction of the bow-fronted sitting-room window of Miss Sayer's cottage at the top of the road. It was a moment or two before Mrs Charles's vision settled and then, pausing to gaze back thoughtfully at the cottage, she could see David Sayer standing in the window and looking through the opera glasses his aunt used on occasion to monitor the comings and goings of her distant neighbours as they went about their daily business. It gave Mrs Charles a very bad feeling.

Pausing momentarily on her porch to scrape some mud from one of the heels of her shoes, she then went inside and put on the kettle for the cup of tea she expected to be offering David within the next fifteen minutes, or however long it took him to walk the distance from his aunt's home to her bungalow.

He arrived less than ten minutes later. The sweaty greyness of his face clearly signalled that he was the bearer of bad news; he had no need to say a word in explanation of what was obviously a pressing need to speak to the clairvoyant. 'We've been summoned: Merton wants to see us ASAP, and by that I mean, something like two hours ago,' he greeted her without preamble. 'It's Linda Kellar, she's dead. Murdered ... committed suicide,' he mumbled, waving a distracted hand in the air. 'Who knows?'

Mrs Charles motioned to him to be seated while she poured tea for the two of them.

'You knew this was going to happen, you've said it all along,' he muttered, nodding his thanks as she passed his tea to him. 'Merton's mad as hell because you were right – I had to tell him that you suspected something like this might happen. Cheryl Baxter is in police custody: she's confessed to killing Linda. They've contacted Linda's brother – he's off somewhere on a weekend work-related course or conference that's been set up by an American company hoping to pinch the best of our brains – and he's on his way back; should be here before nightfall.'

'You said something about suicide, though,' Mrs Charles pointed out with a puzzled frown.

'It's a very confused picture: I would think this is why Clive wants to see you ... us. Cheryl apparently phoned the police from Linda's home which is where, when the boys in blue turned up, they found Linda – in the bathroom, stark naked and very dead in the bathtub. Cheryl was on her knees at the side of the tub, hysterically bawling her eyes out and with one hand clutching one of Linda's, and insisting to all and sundry that she'd killed her, it was all her fault. Linda had apparently been staying with Cheryl for the weekend while her brother is away, but sometime during the night, or early this morning – again this is very confused, Cheryl's not making a lot of sense and has actually had to be sedated – Linda upped and left; went back home without a word to Cheryl. When Cheryl discovered that she'd gone, she went straight round to Linda's place where they either had some sort of row that got seriously out of hand, and Cheryl killed her, as she keeps on insisting, or it wasn't that way at all and she simply found Linda dead in the bath, as I've already said.'

Mrs Charles and David sipped their tea in silence for a few moments. Then Mrs Charles asked, 'Did Mr Merton say how Linda died?'

'It's too early to be certain, but it looks like she drowned after overdosing on paracetamol which she'd washed down with vodka. That's where the possibility of suicide comes in. There was an empty packet of the tablets on a chair in the bathroom along with an empty vodka bottle, and in her free hand, which was submerged in the bath water, she was clutching a photograph of some bloke. Clive said that originally there was some writing on the back of the photograph, but it had been penned in ordinary blue ink which had washed off and was therefore unreadable. Chances are her boyfriend – the bloke in the photo – had told her he was finished with her and she decided to make a proper job of it and finish herself at the same time.'

'The man in the photograph is Andrew Tomlinson,' Mrs Charles informed him quietly.

David stared at her. '*The* Andrew Tomlinson?'

She nodded.

'I'm not going to ask how you know this,' said David. 'I don't think my blood pressure will stand it.' He gave his head a slow shake. 'And God only knows what it will do to Merton's!'

Chapter Fifty-two

'PERHAPS, MADAME, WE COULD BEGIN WITH YOUR EXPLAINING TO ME why the deceased, Linda Kellar, and Cheryl Baxter left your home yesterday afternoon in a severely distressed state,' said Detective Chief Superintendent Merton. He glared at Edwina Charles across his desk: he was furious.

Mrs Charles flicked a quick glance at David Sayer, who occupied a chair to the left of hers. He was gazing steadfastly at his hands which were interlocked on his lap, as if expecting some form of rebuke from her for his having passed this information on to Merton.

'I have really no idea, Mr Merton,' she replied calmly. 'I won't pretend that Linda was in a particularly buoyant frame of mind when we parted, but she was certainly nowhere near as distressed as Mr Sayer apparently observed a short while later.'

'Try using your remarkable powers for seeing things we ordinary mortals can't,' growled Merton, 'and hazard a guess.'

'It may possibly have had something to do with Andrew Tomlinson,' replied Mrs Charles. 'The young man in the photograph that I was given to understand was found by the police clutched in one of Linda's hands ... and, as I am sure you do not need me to remind you, one of the six young people who were at the gravel pit the day Valerie Ward died. Andrew Tomlinson's present whereabouts was the last thing I discussed with Linda moments before she left me yesterday.'

Merton's eyes had narrowed at the mention of Andrew's name. There was a long silence and then he said, 'All right, so it was a photograph of Andrew Tomlinson. Dare I ask how you know this?'

'Linda found it among her mother's possessions,' replied Mrs Charles. 'There was a message on the back of it.'

Merton's eyes narrowed even further and the already high colour of his cheeks darkened ominously. It was late in the day, a few minutes after seven o'clock and still light, but the fluorescent strip above his desk had been switched on, highlighting the sheen of perspiration across his forehead. 'I suppose you know what was in the message?'

'I could hazard a guess, if you like,' she rejoined coolly, and David brought a hand up to his face to cover the small smile that suddenly appeared there.

Merton gave a heavy sigh. 'By all means, please do.'

'Jo Sowerby—' Mrs Charles broke off as Merton leaned forward quickly and then, placing one elbow on his desk, wearily rested his head on his hand.

'Now why aren't I surprised,' he muttered, 'that this was where it was all leading?'

'As I was saying,' continued Mrs Charles, 'Jo Sowerby – who had been in correspondence with Andrew's mother since the Tomlinsons emigrated to New Zealand soon after Valerie Ward died – arranged to meet Andrew, who planned on returning to England. Andrew sent Jo the photograph so that she would recognize him when they met.'

'I hesitate to ask this,' sighed Merton, taking away his hand and looking directly at the clairvoyant, 'but I assume that this was because Jo Sowerby wanted to see him, and for the same reason that she pestered everybody else associated with what had happened to Valerie Ward?'

'No, it was the other way round; Andrew wanted to see her to put an end to the matter once and for all. Had they met as planned, he was going to confess to her that he killed Valerie Ward.'

Merton pinched the skin on the bridge of his nose between a forefinger and thumb. 'Before this goes any further, Madame, I think I should perhaps make it clear to you that in addition to confessing to having killed Linda Kellar, Cheryl Baxter has finally confessed to the murder of Valerie Ward.'

Mrs Charles looked at him for a moment. 'Tell a lie often enough, and in time you'll believe it yourself, Mr Merton,' she said at length.

'All right, all right.' He scowled at her. 'You may have your say. If Andrew Tomlinson murdered Valerie, why would Cheryl Baxter confess to having been the guilty party?'

'Because this was what everyone thought and said, and having had the accusation levelled at her for years, she finally came to believe it herself. Not without good reason, I might add. She did push Valerie into the gravel pit; she thought she probably *had* killed her. But she hadn't, someone else did.'

'Yes, yes; I heard you the first time: Andrew Tomlinson has put up his hands and said he killed her,' said Merton with another sigh.

'By not being there,' said Mrs Charles.

'Pardon me?' said Merton.

'He wasn't there. He said he was, but he wasn't. He left the others and went chasing off after Bernard Watson. Valerie had been making fun of Bernard and Bernard couldn't handle it. He'd got terribly upset and Andrew was worried about him ... what he might do. Bernard was apparently nowhere near as tough as the others and Andrew, who was aware of this, was afraid that Bernard might harm himself. Andrew caught up with him, calmed him down and brought him back. By which time it was all over. Valerie was dead. Cheryl had, in the meantime, come back and told Barry what had happened between her and Valerie at the gravel pit. All this time, the other boy, Jonathon Lewis, was fast asleep. He was the wild one of the group: he'd stolen some cans of lager from the back of a lorry making a delivery to a small convenience store in town and, according to what Andrew has told me, he had got drunk fairly quickly and had passed out even before Andrew had gone off after Bernard. When Andrew and Bernard got back to the others, Jonathon was woken up and then they all started for home which meant their having to pass the gravel pit on the way. This was when they found Valerie dead. Andrew, Bernard and Jonathon kept to the same story that Cheryl had told Barry because it was simpler that way and they saw no reason to dispute it. And this is why Andrew said he killed Valerie ... because as the calm, level-headed one of the six, if he hadn't gone after Bernard and had been there all the time, the chances are that the argument between Valerie and Cheryl wouldn't have got so badly out of hand. Valerie wouldn't have started for home on her own, and Cheryl wouldn't have followed her and continued their squabble at the gravel pit.'

'Look, Madame, this is all very well and good, but aren't you simply confirming what I've been saying?' asked Merton. 'That Cheryl Baxter killed Valerie Ward?'

'For the moment, I am merely repeating what Andrew Tomlinson told me this morning of what he believes would have happened had he been with the others all the time that afternoon. Like you, he has never had any reason to doubt that Cheryl killed Valerie. He has made the same mistake that everyone else, including Cheryl herself, has made. Sadly, it is quite possibly true that had Andrew and Bernard Watson not gone off the way they had and been there to witness exactly what had happened after Cheryl had left Barry and the sleeping Jonathan, to follow Valerie, Valerie would not have been murdered. This wasn't a spur of the moment killing, this was cold-blooded murder, Mr Merton. The problem with Valerie was that she had begun to make a nuisance of herself by telling three of the four males in their little group that I know of for certain, that she was pregnant by them.'

'She wasn't pregnant,' said Merton flatly.

'Yes, so I've been given to understand,' said Mrs Charles. 'But she was a tease, a very silly girl who enjoyed saying things that were untrue and which she knew would upset and worry people. She had, however, almost certainly slept with three of the boys who were with her that afternoon, and so it was not impossible that she was pregnant by one of them. Bernard Watson, the most sensitive of them all, took what she'd told him very seriously. He was infatuated with her and was delighted by the prospect of becoming a father. I have spoken to his sister who has told me that his family believe that this was the motivating factor in his committing suicide after she died. Andrew, though, had Valerie pretty well summed up and took what she said with a pinch of salt. The third boy she'd slept with wasn't taking any chances. He was ambitious, he was going places where a girl like Valerie wouldn't fit in: he had absolutely no intention of getting tied down with her and a baby at fourteen years of age. So he did something about it, Cheryl Baxter very kindly offering him a golden opportunity for taking care of the problem in what was for him the most satisfactory way possible. He followed Cheryl, keeping his distance, and saw exactly what happened between the two girls. Then, when Cheryl started back after having had second thoughts and returning to the gravel pit to make sure that Valerie was all right – and after waiting until she, Cheryl, was safely out of sight – *he* pushed Valerie, who was climbing out of the pit the last time Cheryl saw her, and then he finished the job by scrambling down after her and holding her head under water until she drowned. He and the others drifted back together at more or less the same time, not one of them, allegedly – other than for Cheryl, of course – thinking or knowing that something out of the ordinary had taken place. That discovery, as I've already said, came later on their way home.'

David had raised his head to look at Mrs Charles, switching his gaze to Merton when Merton nodded and said, 'All very plausible, Madame, it could have happened that way, but it didn't. Trust me—'

'No, Mr Merton, you must trust me,' said the clairvoyant. 'You see, I haven't quite finished.'

He sighed. 'I had a feeling there'd be more.'

'I warned Linda to be on her guard,' said Mrs Charles. 'In no circumstances was she to put her trust in someone, a man.'

'We're talking tarot gobbledygook now, are we?' sneered Merton. 'OK, carry on, I'll play along. But let me guess: this Andrew is going to turn out to be the bad guy – I feel it in my waters.'

'Linda certainly went to him during the period that she disappeared and while the police, at the behest of her brother, were searching for her. Andrew gave her sanctuary, if you like, overnight. This was after she'd made her way back to Gidding from Roy Adams's home where she had been held – voluntarily, I might add – after he'd picked her up along the road outside my home following her initial visit to me for a reading of the tarot. Linda heard the shot that killed Roy Adams, but she didn't see who killed him. She panicked when she found his body, and needing time to think and somewhere to stay while she decided what she was going to do about what she knew, she went to Andrew, the young man she had been keeping company with for a short time and knew as Eddie Nuttall. I asked Andrew if Linda had ever confided any of this in him and he said an emphatic no, which meant the danger to her life came from another source.'

Merton and David looked at one another, then at Mrs Charles. They waited.

'There was only one person in whom Linda would confide, totally and without fear, Mr Merton,' she said quietly.

'*Her brother?*' David guessed in a slightly shocked voice, and both Mrs Charles and Merton turned their heads and looked at him thoughtfully.

Chapter Fifty-three

THE SILENCE IN MERTON'S OFFICE WAS OPPRESSIVE AND FROM David's point of view, seemed to last forever.

Embarrassed, he was on the point of apologizing for his having butted in with such a ludicrous suggestion, but was forestalled by Mrs Charles, who said, 'Andrew Tomlinson has arranged with Cheryl to meet her and Barry tomorrow night at their flat – to blackmail them, Cheryl believed. Andrew assures me that this thought has never crossed his mind; he simply wanted to clear up what has since become, to him – and largely due to Jo Sowerby's persistence – a grey area in the statement that he had made to the police all those years ago. He didn't think too much about Jo Sowerby's death – after all, it was widely reported that she'd died of a heart attack. But then when Roy Adams was shot, Andrew started to think the same thing I thought when I heard that Jo Sowerby was dead. What if someone knew that Jo planned on meeting him, Andrew, to discuss Valerie's death? What if that someone had every reason for not only thinking that Roy Adams would know about this, but also for thinking that Roy would become suspicious and take up the cudgel for and on behalf of Jo?'

Mrs Charles saw that she finally had Merton's undivided attention. He was looking at her intently, perhaps not entirely convinced by the argument she was putting forth, but at least he was listening to her.

She continued, 'Hitherto there had never been any question of any of the others from that day at the gravel pit suddenly turning up and causing trouble. Bernard Watson was dead, so was Jonathon Lewis – Andrew's mother had kept in touch with the

Lewises after they'd emigrated to Africa, and she knew that Jonathon had died out there – and Andrew was in New Zealand and very unlikely to return to the UK. Cheryl and Barry were, in effect, all that remained of the original six young people at the gravel pit on the day that Valerie Ward died. Cheryl was no problem, she had always been besotted with Barry, she'd never question him: she would live out the rest of her life, up to a point, wallowing in her misery and content to believe that she'd killed Valerie. She had lived with this notion fixed firmly in her head for so long that it had become a permanent part of her life. Barry, of course, was only too happy to let her get on with it.'

'My God, Madame,' said Merton. 'You're surely not suggesting that it was Barry Kellar who "mugged" – no doubt with intention to kill – his mother?'

Mrs Charles widened her eyes as him questioningly. 'Why wouldn't Jo tell him that she was going to meet Andrew? It was largely on Barry's behalf that she was carrying out her vendetta against Cheryl. Barry would also have known that she would take Roy Adams into her confidence about Andrew's return. So first Barry killed his mother, or attempted to kill her – and what makes me so sure of this is something that Linda told me … information she deliberately withheld from the police at the time of her mother's death.'

Merton's eyes narrowed balefully. 'Withholding vital evidence, may I remind you, Madame, is a criminal offence. Not that I would expect for one moment that it would have in any way altered our official findings in regard to Jo Sowerby's death.'

'That, Mr Merton, is a moot point,' responded Mrs Charles calmly. 'According to Linda, her mother never went anywhere near her father's grave, the place where the police claim that Jo was attacked. This means that she was attacked somewhere else and then left at the grave where the evidence was found and which pointed to the attack on her having taken place there.'

Merton drew in his breath, held on to it for a moment and then he said, 'So where precisely was she attacked – or is this pure speculation, the fantasizing of an immature young girl?'

'I don't think so,' said Mrs Charles. 'From what Linda has told me of her mother's habits – and this is what Linda herself believes – Jo was attacked on the opposite side of the cemetery, at the graveside of Valerie and her mother, where Jo often went late at night after her shift at the pub, to talk to them about her quest for justice for Valerie's death.'

'I suppose there is a point to all of this?' said Merton, scowling at her. 'Some reason why it was there and not where we found the evidence that proved beyond a shadow of doubt that it was at her late first husband's graveside that she was attacked?'

Mrs Charles nodded. 'Barry couldn't risk having his mother found anywhere near Valerie's grave after he'd attacked her: it could all too easily have opened up the Ward case again. So he faked the evidence you, the police, discovered at his father's grave. This was something he was eminently skilled at, a passion of his: forensics. Where some young college students will spend their annual break from college, or gap year, backpacking in Australia or Thailand, he spent his busily gaining work experience in a forensic laboratory. I believe you will find it on record that it was while he was employed there that he was fined for a minor traffic offence.'

As the one who had supplied Mrs Charles with this information in regard to Barry Kellar's employment at the time of the driving offence, David Sayer held his breath, waiting for some challenge from Merton, but the moment passed and Mrs Charles continued.

'Before that, he was working for Morgan Kempthorne & Sons, the Gidding funeral directors. Barry knew exactly what the police would look for and how to fake that evidence convincingly. Barry's abiding interest is in forensic science – it always has been. It is what he has been doing this weekend, as the guest of a prestigious American company seeking to recruit new scientific staff. Also, if you check with Mrs Kempthorne, I am sure she will confirm that it was Barry Kellar who borrowed – for want of a better word – the funeral car that turned up at the children's birthday party held by the Baxters, and if you contact the florist, Joyce Cooper, she will likewise confirm that it was Barry who came into her shop and paid for the floral tributes that were delivered to the Baxters' home that same day. All on behalf of his mother, of course. I don't for one moment think that any of this was Barry's idea—'

'All fine and dandy, most convincing,' Merton cut in. 'I do hope, though, that you're not suggesting we reopen the Ward case and charge Barry Kellar with Valerie's murder. We wouldn't have a hope of bringing him to book after all this time.'

'Nor for his sister's murder,' Mrs Charles agreed with a nod. 'He's far too clever to leave any trace of himself that would tie him in with her death. But he killed her, Mr Merton: he was the man the tarot warned would be a threat to Linda's life if she confided in him. My guess is that she waited until Cheryl was asleep last night, and then she phoned her brother and told him that she thought she should go to the police and tell them that their mother never went near their father's grave. By then, Linda would have been in a very distressed state and Barry didn't dare risk trying to calm her down over the phone. I think he slipped out of the hotel where he had been staying over the weekend and came back home, met Linda, as arranged, at their mother's home, and sadly, it all came out … everything. That she knew their mother would never have been attacked anywhere near their father's grave, that she had been at Roy Adams's home the day he was shot, that she had discovered that her boyfriend, Eddie, was the man in the photograph she had found among their mother's things, that his real name is Andrew, and that he had planned on meeting their mother. Barry would have seen his hopes and dreams slipping swiftly away from him. Linda knew too much; she didn't fully appreciate that herself, but this was the reality. She had become a danger to him – more so than his mother or Roy Adams had ever been. They had unwittingly only ever played into his hands with their obsessive belief in Cheryl's guilt; and so somehow, he got his sister to swallow enough paracetamol tablets – perhaps in a hot drink – to make her drowsy, and then he set the scene in the bathroom for her apparent suicide.'

Merton was thoughtful. 'Fair enough; we should be able to prove that Linda phoned him, but that doesn't mean he came back and killed her. It's all pure speculation, Madame.'

'I agree,' said Mrs Charles. 'If you can't find a witness who saw him leaving the conference hotel late last night, or someone who saw him near his mother's home later on, then I dare say that proving he killed his sister would be very difficult for you. He's been quite clever. But not quite clever enough. He's made one mistake. He probably knows this by now, but is keeping his fingers crossed that no one will ever spot it.'

'And that is?' asked Merton.

Mrs Charles was quiet for a moment. Then she said, 'I owe it to Linda, and even more so to Cheryl for all the years she's spent agonizing over Valerie Ward, to make sure that Barry Kellar pays for at least one of the four crimes he has committed. Cheryl won't thank me for it, of course – I accept that. However, there is a distinct possibility that maybe one day, Barry will see even her as a threat and decide to get rid of her, too. I am almost certain this is exactly what will happen and this is why I must try and do what I can now to save her, as was the case with Linda, from herself.'

'Go on, I'm listening,' said Merton.

'As I've already said, Cheryl believes that Andrew Tomlinson is a blackmailer. I'm quite sure she has already confided this in Barry. Carry through with this fiction, Mr Merton. Arrange with Andrew to keep his appointment with them.'

Merton looked at her. 'And?'

'I will give you the evidence that you need to arrest and charge Barry Kellar with murder,' Mrs Charles promised him.

Chapter Fifty-four

BARRY KELLAR SHOOK HANDS WITH ANDREW TOMLINSON ENTHUSI-astically. 'Good to see you,' he said. 'Go on through to the living-room.' He pointed to an open doorway at the end of the hallway, and then waved Andrew on ahead of him. 'You'll find Cheryl in there.'

Cheryl looked up at the two men nervously as they entered the room. She was very pale with dark smudges under her sunken eyes from lack of sleep. She felt confused and deeply distressed; had no idea what was going on. One minute she was on the point of being charged with Linda's murder, the next she was being told she could go home. She had asked Barry to deal with Andrew and his anticipated blackmail threat on his own, but Barry had laughed off her request and told her that she was being extremely silly, and that Andrew's hint of blackmail was either all in her imagination or a bluff. Cheryl couldn't explain it, but the feeling that Andrew had the power somehow to destroy them both persisted to the point where when she finally faced him across the room, she thought she was going to faint.

'I was going to phone back and cancel when I read about Linda in the paper this morning,' said Andrew in an apologetic voice. He looked at Barry and Cheryl in turn. 'It was such a shock: I really am very sorry; you must be devastated.' He sounded uncomfortable and felt awkward; thought it showed.

Barry frowned. 'My fault, I hadn't realized how vulnerable and fragile she was. Our mother's death obviously upset her a great deal more than either Cheryl or I had suspected.'

'It was suicide, then?' asked Andrew tentatively.

Cheryl had been staring at him fixedly. She had to look away for fear that she would say something she'd regret. She had never hated anyone as much in all her life, not even Valerie. She just wished he'd get on with it, say what he had to say and go.

Barry made a dismissive gesture with one hand. 'We'll know more after the post-mortem has been carried out: but that's how it looks; she overdosed and then drowned in the bathtub.'

'I'm sorry,' Andrew said again.

Liar! Cheryl wanted to shout at him. But she remained silent: Barry had told her to leave this to him.

Abruptly, Barry changed the subject and began chatting easily with Andrew about Andrew's life in the Antipodes and how he himself was seriously considering accepting an offer of a job which would involve a move to America. Cheryl took no part in the conversation: listening to them made her want to scream. Neither man seemed in any hurry to get to the point and discuss the reason for Andrew's visit. She couldn't believe it when Barry suggested opening a bottle of wine to mark the occasion of their reunion after all these years.

She shook her head at the glass Barry offered her. She could stand it no longer. 'Stop it,' she said in a shaky voice. 'Both of you! Linda finally told me on Saturday about how she's been seeing you, Andrew – or should that be Eddie?' she asked him in a bitter voice – 'and that Barry's mother had contacted you about Valerie.'

The muscles in Cheryl's throat constricted: she thought she was going to choke and had to swallow several times to try and ease the pain there. It took her a moment or two to compose herself. Her eyes were bright and shiny with the threat of tears. 'Well, bad luck, Andrew; you're too late. I've confessed to the police that I killed Valerie. You've had a wasted journey.'

He looked surprised. 'I never thought there was any question about it. I mean, I thought the police have always known that you killed her. The rest of us certainly did.' He looked at Barry. 'Didn't we?' he asked him.

Cheryl and Barry looked at one another. 'Well, why did you want to see us … me?' she demanded, coming back to Andrew.

'And don't tell me it was for old times' sake!' There was a note of hysteria creeping into her voice. 'You know as well as I do that all of you were glad to see the back of me after what happened at the gravel pit that day – even Barry steered clear of me for a time. So why would you suddenly want to renew your acquaintance with me, with either of us, for that matter, if you've always believed that I killed Valerie? She was your friend; you must still feel something over what happened to her, even after all this time.'

Andrew had drained his glass. He held it out for a refill. He couldn't bring himself to look at either one of them. It came as a shock to admit this to himself, but for the first time he felt genuinely sorry for Cheryl. She was only a young woman, but what he saw before him at the moment was pathetic: her sunken eyes and the pale flesh on her face, which was drawn taut over her cheekbones, had given her head a skull-like appearance. She looked old and defeated and he despised Barry, someone he had always looked up to, for his hand in making her what she had become.

'Actually,' he said after a moment, 'I hardly ever think of Valerie: I would probably have never given what happened to her any thought if it hadn't been for your mother, Barry, forever going on to my mother about it. Why would I?' He widened his eyes at the two of them and then went on, 'Although I must admit that sometimes I've wished I'd been straight with the police at the time about my exact whereabouts while you were off having your little tiff with her, Cheryl. We all know I wasn't there, don't we? Neither was Bernard, and as for poor old Jonathon … well, forget it! He was so out of it, he wouldn't have known what day of the week it was.' He waved a hand nonchalantly in the air. 'Not that it would have made any difference then, and particularly not now. You've confessed, Cheryl: end of!'

Where Cheryl had moments before been merely pale, she was now the colour of best bone china. She looked at Barry. 'I don't feel very well, I think I should go and lie down for a while. As there is nothing more to be said, I think you should ask Andrew to leave.'

'Yes, you run along, pet,' said Andrew. He spoke sympatheti-
cally. 'It wasn't you I really wanted to see, anyway. I wanted to
talk to Barry about Roy Adams.'

'He's dead,' said Cheryl with a puzzled frown. 'Someone shot
him.'

'I know,' said Andrew. There was a small amount of liquid in
the bottom of his glass and he gazed at it, hoping to conceal his
growing unease over the situation in which he had been
persuaded by Edwina Charles to place himself, and wondering if
he were going to be able to bring it off. 'Linda was there, at his
home, the day he was shot.'

There was a stunned silence. Cheryl was staring so hard at
Andrew that the strain on her eyeballs was becoming unbearable.
Then Barry laughed. 'Nonsense, Linda would never go anywhere
near Roy Adams. She couldn't stand the sight of him. Neither of
us could for what he did to our mother. It was thanks to him that
she obsessed the way she did over Valerie.'

Cheryl looked at Barry, then back at Andrew. Her voice
reflected her bewilderment. 'Linda shot Roy? Is that what you
want us to believe?'

'I really have no idea, pet,' said Andrew. 'All I know is that she
bundled the bloodstained clothes the shooter wore – and presumably, that was her, who else would it have been? – into a black
plastic bin bag and then she dumped it in the river. I followed her
and retrieved it.'

Barry looked at him expressionlessly. 'Why?'

'Why?' echoed Andrew. He contrived to look puzzled. His eyes
widened; he gave a slight shrug. 'Because I thought you should
know what I'd found and do something about it. I know I could
have left the bag where I found it, but I was curious and now,
unfortunately, I'm stuck with it. What worries me is that if I try
to get rid of it and someone sees me doing so, I could find myself
in dead trouble. Linda's gone, Barry: there's no point in dragging
her and you, her family, through any more mud over what
happened to Valerie. And that's what this is all about, isn't it?
Valerie again. But the fact remains that I've got the bag and
what's in it, and now I don't know what to do about it. I don't

want to get involved. Do you understand what I'm saying, Barry? I hate to dump this on you, but this is your problem: Linda was your sister; you sort it.'

'Where is this bag now?' asked Barry coolly.

'Outside … in my car,' replied Andrew. 'I was hoping you'd take if off me and do whatever's necessary.'

'Don't!' said Cheryl sharply, as Barry put down his glass, as if ready to do Andrew's bidding.

Barry said, 'I must. For Linda's sake, Cheryl. Andrew's right. Enough's enough. It ends here. I'll get rid of it safely. No one outside of we three need ever know that she was involved in Roy's shooting.'

Andrew saw the light of battle begin to shine in Cheryl's eyes. She was suspicious, nowhere near done. 'And me,' he reminded her quickly. 'It's not just Linda who's involved here. I've handled the bag, haven't I? My fingerprints will be all over it. At least, I imagine so. I'm not like you, Barry: what do I know about forensics? I just want shut of the bag. As quickly as possible.'

Barry indicated to Andrew to lead the way out of the flat. 'Thanks, Barry,' said Andrew as they went down the stairs to the street. 'I owe you.'

He tried his best not to feel a Judas as he opened the boot of his car, then dragged out the bin bag and handed it to Barry.

'Don't ever come near either one of us ever again; never get in contact with us again,' Barry warned him. 'This is goodbye.'

'And good luck to you, too, mate,' murmured Andrew under his breath, as Barry turned to face the plainclothes detectives who had quietly approached them in the company of two uniformed police officers.

All of them heard Cheryl scream out Barry's name. She had been standing at the living-room window, watching what was happening in the street below; saw the approach of the police officers and knew instinctively that Barry had walked into a trap.

She ran wildly from the flat and then down the stairs and out into the street. The police officers couldn't understand a word of what she screeched at them. Only Andrew and her fiancé had an inkling of what she might have said, which ran something along the lines of: '*Arrest me. I'm the one. It's because of what I did to Valerie that day at the gravel pit. I killed them, I killed them all.*' And then she collapsed at their feet.

Chapter Fifty-five

DAVID SAYER WAS WAITING FOR EDWINA CHARLES AS SHE CAME OUT of the Post Office Stores several days later. He was in a sombre mood as they started slowly along the road towards her bungalow.

'The blood on the clothing in the bin bag you and Andrew Tomlinson found is definitely Roy Adams's,' he said. 'I thought you'd like to know.'

'And the jeans and T-shirt ... were they Barry's?' she asked.

He nodded. 'He's been formally charged with Roy Adams's murder. He's denying it, of course – claims somebody stole his jeans and T-shirt, shot Roy Adams and then tried to frame him by leaving them in his late mother's washing machine. I would imagine his aim was for his sister to pile in a load more laundry without taking much notice, if any, of the soiled clothing that was already in there, and then give the lot a good wash. He has no explanation for why Linda should think his things should be disposed of the way they were, and again he's twisted everything round by insisting that this proves his sister was mentally unstable and hence her suicide. He's also turned things a bit on their head by pointing the finger at Andrew Tomlinson as being the most likely person to try and frame him. Barry's got all the answers – thinks he has, anyway.'

Mrs Charles looked at him thoughtfully. 'What reason would Andrew have for trying to do something like that to him?'

'Barry's doing his level best to link everything to Valerie Ward's death at the gravel pit. Unfortunately for Andrew, he reminded Barry that he wasn't on the scene all the time that day, and now Barry questions whether it was Andrew and not Cheryl who killed Valerie. Barry's a devious customer, all right. But so is Merton. He'll get him. Merton's got a team checking on Barry's comings and goings on the night his sister died. Strictly off the record, they've got one witness who is quite positive that she saw Barry leaving the hotel and getting into his car at around eleven o'clock that night.... A lady of the night – a high-class call girl who was leaving her client at the hotel even more discreetly than Barry left it. Then not long after this, there was an incident at a motorway service station while Barry was pulling in to refuel. A car following his came off the motorway too fast and its driver lost control on a curve, hitting a wall and lightly clipping the rear of Barry's car. The damage was pretty insignificant, but the police were called out to the scene because there was a suggestion that the other driver had been drinking. The police had to cart him off to hospital to be breathalysed: they didn't have a kit with them. Barry's been identified by the two motorway coppers involved and also by the girl at the desk in the service station. He paid by cash; was smart enough not to use any cards, but she's recognized him from a photograph she's been shown. So one way or another, Merton will get him – thanks to Andrew Tomlinson, and you, of course, for taking the trouble to find the bin bag that Linda dumped.'

'Cyril, actually,' she confessed with a smile. 'All Andrew and I did was get our footwear – light sandals in Andrew's case – a little bit muddied on the river-bank. It was Cyril who went into the river and unhooked the bag from a half submerged branch of a tree. He wasn't best pleased about it, either. He was wearing new shoes which he couldn't take off in case he trod on some broken glass or some other sharp object that he couldn't see in the muddied water. There was quite a lot of broken glass here and there along the river-bank; it would have been very risky to wade in after the bag, barefoot.'

They walked in silence for a few moments. Then Mrs Charles said, 'I've been worried about Cheryl. Do you know how she's coping?'

'By all accounts, very badly. Her doctor has had her admitted to hospital: she is apparently suffering from a severe nervous breakdown.'

'I'm very sorry to hear that, but not surprised,' admitted Mrs Charles. 'She'd been carrying a terrible load for many years and the sudden realization that there was every possibility that she was innocent, she didn't kill Valerie, would have come as a terrible shock to her. Sadly, it was all going to end in tears: there was no marriage indicated in her reading.'

'You'd told her this?'

'No.' Mrs Charles shook her head. 'There were much bigger issues at stake.' She was quiet for a moment. 'So much depended on Linda, on whether she would heed my warning and not confide in the man whom I knew would threaten and very possibly, take her life.'

'Which the silly girl didn't do.'

'The fact that I could see no wedding bells in Cheryl's future was a fairly strong indication that Linda would make that fatal mistake. Understandable, of course: as it turned out, the man in question was her brother. It would never have crossed her mind that he was not to be trusted. I failed, I didn't see this possibility. It would have puzzled me, anyway: I saw no reason to suspect him, and Linda, to a large extent, was her own enemy by withholding that one vital piece of information about where she believed her mother had been attacked in the cemetery. Had she confided this in me earlier, it would have altered her reading and not impossibly, given me a clear indication of the man's identity.'

'Well, it's as Jean used to say to me way back when I was a copper and I knew damn well that I'd collared the right villain for a crime, but couldn't prove it.... You can't win them all!'

'One thing that has puzzled me,' confessed Mrs Charles, 'is how Barry got hold of Roy Adams's shotgun. I was given to understand that Roy's home wasn't broken into, and surely he wasn't in the habit of leaving the weapon lying about outside the house for someone – Barry – to find and use.'

'The answer to whether or not Roy left the weapon lying about is yes and no. It should, by law, have been kept under lock and key in the cabinet that he keeps for the purpose up in his loft. However, the only time it is up there, is when he's been given the nod by a friend at the nick that he's about to receive another of the prescribed visits from the law to make sure that it is being kept securely in its proper place. The rest of the time, he kept it in his living-room, near the patio door and within easy reach for his regular afternoon sessions of taking pot shots at wild birds. At the time of the shooting, Roy was in dispute over a rear window which a local company had recently fitted, and which Roy claimed to be of inferior quality and had insisted should be replaced. The company had taken out the disputed window and in the meanwhile, had left the opening boarded up with a sheet of chipboard. It would have been relatively easy to remove the board to gain access to the house; it was only meant to remain in place for a day or two. This is the theory that Merton's working on at present, anyway – that Barry removed the board and climbed in through the opening, got hold of Roy's shotgun, then climbed back out, boarding up the opening behind him and then waiting on the patio for Roy to return home.'

'I wish Mr Merton luck,' said Mrs Charles musingly. 'I think he might be going to need all he can get in his dealings with that particular young man.'

'Kellar's a slippery customer, all right,' David conceded.

They had reached the clairvoyant's bungalow and pausing at the gate, David said, 'My reason for tracking you down in the village was to let you know that Jean and I will be returning to our own home this evening. Aunt Margaret's doctor has given her the all clear. I personally don't think there was ever anything much wrong with her except an acute attack of lonelyitis. I couldn't have taken much more of her company, anyway. She's driving me crazy. One of her friends, Molly Pearson, popped round a short while ago with news of Stan North's hunt for a woolly bear – of all things! – in her garden. Molly and my aunt think this proves beyond a shadow of doubt what they've always thought about Stan – that he's completely bonkers, a danger to the community and should be rounded up and locked away. Woolly bears!' David exclaimed with a laugh. 'Where on earth do the silly old dears get these ideas?'

Mrs Charles looked at him solemnly. 'There have actually been a number of reported sightings of a woolly bear in and around the village over the past few days. Mr North is in my back garden at the moment – at least he was there when I left an hour ago to go into the village. He's mounting guard on the woolly bear he found there first thing this morning to make sure no harm comes to it.'

David looked at her. 'I've got to see this,' he said. 'A woolly bear? On the loose and not caged up in a zoo?'

'A woolly bear,' she assured him with a solemn nod.

Bemused, David followed her to where Stan North was sitting in a striped canvas deckchair on her back lawn. An empty coffee mug lay on its side on the ground beside the chair. He didn't look round at their approach.

Mrs Charles said, 'Mr Sayer has come to see our precious woolly bear, Mr North.'

Stan North sprung up out of the chair like a Jack in the Box and pointed to a bare patch of lawn where the larva of the Garden Tiger Moth was busily munching its way through a plantain.

'A caterpillar?' David looked at Mrs Charles incredulously.

'A *woolly bear* caterpillar,' Mrs Charles corrected him. She would like to have added that she was delighted that one had actually been found in *her* garden, thereby justifying the deception she had employed in an endeavour to restore Stan North's reputation and bring him safely back into the community. This, however, was best kept a secret between her and her conscience. She only wished the outcome of the gift that Jo Sowerby had made to Cheryl Baxter of a reading of the tarot had had a similar happy outcome. Jo Sowerby had been granted her wish: her gift of a tarot reading had ultimately unmasked Valerie Ward's killer. But at what a cost!

Stan North gave them both a severe look. 'The larva of an *Arctia caja*,' he reprimanded them. His expression changed markedly as his eyes suddenly lit up. His voice became earnest. 'It flies in July and August, Mr Sayer. It used to be quite common hereabouts, but has been in serious decline for some years now.'

David flicked a sidelong glance at Mrs Charles before leaning forward and endeavouring to look impressed by what was obviously a welcome reappearance of this particular many-legged, herbaceous plant muncher which, all being well, would shortly metamorphose into a winged insect and take flight. 'Fascinating,' he said.